THE SCRIBE

After the crucifixion of Jesus, the aftermath and birth of the gospel writers

Liam Robert Mullen

Liam Robert Mullen

Copyright © 2016 Liam Robert Mullen

All rights reserved.

No part of this book may be reproduced, or stored in a retrieval system, or transmitted in any form or by any means, electronic, mechanical, photocopying, recording, or otherwise, without express written permission of the publisher.

ISBN-13: 9798833266571

Cover design by: John Lutheran The Book Cover Designer
Library of Congress Control Number: 2018675309
Printed in the United States of America

This book is dedicated to my parents Tony and Marie Mullen. It is also dedicated to my brother Tony for his often invaluable help especially computer matters which are apt to drive me up the wall.

CHAPTER 1.

30 AD.

Thunder and lightning lashed the city of Jerusalem. The storm broke with a fury unparalleled in the lifetimes of all those present, and people grew afraid. Even the Roman soldiers, hardened as they were by army life and accustomed to a life of battle and bloodshed, threw nervous glances at the sky.

The sky was a cauldron of angry colours - dark orange, purples, raw sienna, ochre yellows, black and greys, and pierced by giant streaks of jagged white lightning. There was a roar in the air, as though a giant breath of anger had been unleashed. Dark grey cloud scudded across the sky, and the land itself grew dark. The sun was gone, replaced not with a wonderful night sky of moon and stars, but by a malevolent scowl of the harshest weather anyone present had ever seen. There was a biting coldness in the air, and the people accustomed as they were to a warm Mediterranean climate, shivered uncontrollably.

Rain had begun to fall, sheets of angry little pellets that stung the faces of the people. Many turned towards home, but more than a few threw a backwards glance to the limp figure hanging on the cross whom they had earlier mocked. They weren't laughing now. Instead, their faces were contorted with a baffled puzzlement and no little fear.

One citizen, normally a quiet reserved man screamed at those members of the Sanhedrin still left: "You brought this," he screamed at them. "You brought this...this wrath. This wrath of

God."

They stared at him in silence. Sullen.

Escobar scowled and turned away. In his early thirties, he had been persuaded by the arguments of the High Priest Ciaiphas to condemn the young man who hung limply on the cross, and until this moment had felt no compunction or guilt at his decision. What had moved him was the dignity of the man as he died on the cross. The man's demeanour had been different than the two thieves who hung either side of him. The voice had held an air of reverence that Escobar had been intrigued by, and for the first time he had looked inward and recognised his own weaknesses. A gnawing doubt engulfed his very being, and his thin face convulsed with the realisation that he might have been wrong. Had he been too quick to judge, to condemn, to nurture favour with Ciaiphas and other senior members of the Sanhedrin?

Escobar didn't know.

What he did know was that in the last hour his beliefs had been shaken to his very core, and he knew in an instant that everything had changed. Everything had changed, and yet nothing had changed. He was confused by his sudden change of heart. He'd seen other crucifixions and couldn't understand why this one had moved him so deeply.

He gazed up at the man on the cross, his brown eyes suddenly moist, as though the dead Galilean could supply an answer. But the lips of the man were now silent, a thin trickle of blood coursing the sides of a still countenance strangely at peace. A crown of thorns still clung to the matted hair and a sign above the man's head bore evidence of his supposed crime. It read simply: INRI.

King of the Jews. Roman parlance. Roman humour.

Escobar suddenly realised that the rain had merged with the dead man's blood and had washed around his sandaled feet. He moved back, still mesmerised by the face of the man on the cross, unheeding of the rain which lashed his face. He could hear sobbing nearby, and turning he recognised the dead man's mother. She had been pointed out to him earlier in the day. Pity engulfed him, and for a moment he wanted to go to her and embrace her.

A man was with her - another Galilean. He held her in the embrace that Escobar had wanted to give. For a moment, the two men locked eyes. Escobar saw the grief in the man's eyes and turned away. A friend, obviously. Other women were nearby, also sobbing.

Unnerved, Escobar began moving away. He had never been comfortable in the grief shown by women. He moved slowly, his steps hesitant. Looking around, he saw that most people had now left. The soldiers had left.

The sky was still accentuated with the sounds of fierce lightning and wind shear. It was beginning to ease somewhat, as the executioners took down the bodies of the three men on the crosses. Escobar walked back through the narrow empty alleyways of the Holy City towards the temple. He became aware of a commotion there.

Entering he stopped dead.

The temple looked like it had been hit with an earthquake. The words of the man who had died came back and haunted him: "Destroy this temple, and in three days I'll raise it again."

Escobar shivered. He could see Ciaiphas shaking his head in

disbelief and the whispered mutterings of others.

"An earthquake?" one man suggested.

"Nonsense," replied his companion.

"Then what?"

"Him."

Escobar followed their gaze. The bodies had been removed, but the three crosses were still visible on the summit of Mount Calvary. He shivered again. His eyes fell on the broken alabaster littering the stone floor and moved to the heavy curtain that had split in two, its heavy lace dangling like a man on a cross. Stonework had cracked and broke. He coughed as dust hit his lungs.

He wondered what Rachel would have made of it. She had been his constant companion since his early teen years, but she had died when she was expecting their first child. The baby hadn't survived either.

"Complications," they had said.

Though gone two years, Escobar still missed Rachel as though she had died only yesterday. The love of his life had been snatched cruelly from his life, leaving only bitterness in its wake. He had struggled with life since.

Every day was an effort.

He'd thrown himself into his work.

An ardent follower of the Sanhedrin, his work had allowed his mind to escape the mind-numbing pain of Rachel's loss, but he still found it a difficult uphill struggle. Up to now he had never questioned his convictions, but now he found himself wondering if others had taken advantage of his circumstances. He sensed Rachel wouldn't have approved of some of his Sanhedrin duties and the people he now associated with. She had been a simple, good woman.

She would have instantly spotted the goodness in the man - Jesus. She had been that kind of woman. Sensing the good in people.

She had abhorred violence. She would have been appalled by the way a convicted murderer like Barabbas had been freed in order to condemn the young Galilean preacher.

Escobar could sense the truth of that. He turned to go.

He needed time alone.

Time to reflect.

Time to pause.

Time to take a long hard look at his life and what he had become. He left the temple and the grim forebodings of the men gathered there and walked slowly home. His mind was busy, thoughtful.

***

Sleep didn't come easy that Friday night.

Escobar turned and tossed, the sheets slick and wet against his body. Nightmares dogged his every breath. His breathing was laboured and shallow. He cried out in fear...naked, dogged fear.

Sheer terror.

A heavy weight was on his chest. He felt like an Egyptian

slave forced to quarry heavy rock, pyramid rock, under the malevolent and baleful gaze of a Pharaoh's lifelong vision. He couldn't move.

He felt paralysed.

The heavy rocks became like giant boulders of durable granite, weighing him down, pinning him, crushing the life out of him. The fear woke him out of a deep slumber. He stumbled blindly from his bed, his throat dry and acrid, his bony fingers reaching for a lantern. He lit the lantern with a tiny flicker of flame that still burned in the hearth. The room lit up slowly.

He brushed his fingers through his lank black hair. His breathing was somewhat easier, and he filled a cup with water from a pail that rested near the doorway. He munched slowly on a piece of flat bread as he went through the doorway and breathed in the night air. The stars shone in abundance, and a half-crescent moon hung low in the sky. He stared at the sky for a long time.

His mood was pensive. Sombre.

Sighing he returned to his quarters.

Everything had changed.

CHAPTER 2.

11 AD.

The Jacob and the Abraham pitched violently in the swell. The winds had come sweeping down from the low-lying hills without warning. What had been a calm swell before now resembled a tempest. Water surged over the bows of the boat, frightening the fishermen.

Water!

Simone saw his grandfather turn to him with a grimace of concern etched on his craggy features. "I don't like the look of this sea, Simone."

The boy nodded at his grandfather in agreement. "The nets are stored away," he shouted back. "Let's head for shore."

His grandfather nodded.

Simone was a sturdy boy for fourteen, with the round shoulders of a Galilean fisherman. He had bright blue eyes like his father and was just beginning to let a beard grow.

All the men were dark tanned, and some had even fished the Mediterranean off to the east. They all knew a bad spell when they saw one. As a boy, Simone had often watched his grandfather set sail, a grin as wide as the blue waters, on those familiar features.

To the young boy, who knew one day he'd follow his grandfather's footsteps, there was always a spirit of adventure and excitement on the faces of those who set out. They always set out at evening time, because even the smallest boy in the village knew the fish rose to the surface at night, when they figured they were safe from the illuminating light of the sunrays and the dives of birds.

Simone was tall for his age, taller than most from his village. His arms were already developing strong muscles from hauling on the nets and dragging the tilapia into the boat. Like all the men of the region he wore a long gown decorated with the tallith. His footwear consisted of leather sandals.

The boats would return at dawn and the happiest memories were always when they'd caught a good catch, and the women would laugh and cry openly, that their men folk were back safe and sound. The children would laugh too, and like children everywhere would get caught up in the excitement, and generally get in the way of things until one of the elders would give a half-clout. Half in exasperation and half good-humoured spirits. At such times even Matthew - the tax collector - would wear a grin on his features.

Sometimes too the boats came back empty, but Simone understood it was the way of the sea. Sometimes they'd pray in the synagogue for a good catch. God would provide.

Suddenly a giant wave crashed over both boats, and Simone sensed, rather than saw men go overboard. He nearly went himself, but the thong on his sandal caught on a boathook and that saved him. His quick thinking enabled him to catch hold of the sail rigging and he clung tightly to it until the giant wave had subsided.

His wide eyes found his grandfather struggling in the water.

"Grandfather," he yelled. "Hang on." Terror clung to his voice like an oily fish. Astounded by the ferocity of the Galilee, he reached out his hand and found his grandfather's arm.

However, his grip wasn't a good one, and bodies immersed in water were always slippery. He could do nothing as his grandfather slowly slipped away from him.

His grandfather caught his eye, and his yell was barely discernible before he slipped beneath the waves. "Save yourself boy. Save the men. I'm lost."

Simone let out an anguished howl of despair. Of all the men dragged overboard from the Jacob only two managed to clamber back aboard. Simone helped them aboard and all three tried to round the boat to help save the others. But it was a lost cause. They'd all sunk beneath the turbulent waves.

Aboard the Jacob, Simone thought of the Chief Rabbi. The story of how Moses had parted the Red Sea with a staff. He wished he had such a staff that would part the Sea of Galilee and allow them safe passage back to land. But such thinking was dangerous. He had to concentrate on the task ahead and not allow his head to be distracted by such tales.

He wasted no time on tears.

They would come later. In the meantime, he aimed to carry out his grandfather's last command: Save himself and as many as the other men as he could.

He signalled the Abraham closer. It too had lost men overboard. Three of its men had been swept away. Without any ado the three survivors from the Jacob climbed aboard the Abraham, and the Jacob was abandoned to the sea.

Oftentimes the Sea of Galilee was a stunning, wild and beautiful place but because of its position deep in the Rift Valley, some two hundred and fifty feet below sea-level, sudden draughts of cold air could sweep in from the low-lying hills and whip the water into a sudden frenzy.

Eight men in one boat had a better chance of survival.

Simone shouted directions, willing and pushing the oarsmen with his harsh orders. Speaking in Hebrew he cursed the weather and cajoled the men to greater efforts. Muscles bulging, and their faces wrought with fatigue, the men struggled to stay alive. To survive they battled towards the nearest land. Capernaum was now out of the question. The men pulled on the oars with the strength of Roman galley slaves, and they used brute strength on the oars to carve a wake through the turbulence.

For a long moment as they got into the shallows, nobody moved. The men hunched over their oars, heads bent, struggling to catch their breaths. They were wet and cold. Struggling ashore, they heaved their boat onto the sand, the wind and rain hampering their every movement. They flopped exhausted on the deserted beach, having dragged the Abraham to a safe spot.

The men found a cave. Simone despatched two of the men to find some driftwood. Two others came back with stones. A fire was built, and the men huddled around it, each silent in their own thoughts. All had lost friends tonight. Good companions whom they had fished and laughed with. Simone himself was haunted by the events of the night. His thoughts wandered…

From an early age Simone had been steeped in the ways of the Synagogue. He had been born in 3 BC. The piety of even the men folk had always intrigued him. The whisper of fervent prayer throughout the mud-bricked building always carried with it the promise of something special, like the scent of a woman's perfume carried on the night wind. He thought again of the Chief Rabbi...happier times...safer times.

Oftentimes the Chief Rabbi would gather the young boys around him and amuse them with fascinating tales. He'd tell them tales of slavery in Egypt where the Pharaohs ruled with a mighty fist and of how Moses had led the people to the Promised Land. The story of Moses had always intrigued young Simone. It sounded incredible!

A baby left to float in a hand-woven basket along the papyrus reed-banked and alligator infested waters of the Nile. The discovery of the baby by a princess who reared him to be a king. The discovery of his real identity and left stranded in the desert to die. But Moses had triumphed over the desert. For years he had wandered, living a nomad existence in that country known as the Sinai. Finally of how his constant search led him face to face with God who gave him a special task. He was appointed to lead the people to the Promised Land.

Moses had gone back to the Pharaoh, stronger and bolder than before. "Let my people go," he'd boomed. To Simone the words had a magic ring about them. The heart of the Pharaoh had hardened though, and he refused to release the Israelites. Simone and the other boys had listened spellbound as they heard how God had unleashed the seven plagues.

Then they heard that the Pharaoh had at last yielded to the requests of Moses - and the Israelites were allowed to go. But the Pharaoh was unhappy later and he mustered his army in pursuit of the fleeing Israelites. With their backs to the Red Sea the Israelites had nowhere left to run, but God commanded Moses: "Lift up your staff and I will push back the waters so that you can lead the people safely across." The people escaped through the two walls of water and when the Egyptian armies tried to follow suit the waters enveloped them, and they were no more.

Simone shook himself from his stupor. There was still much to do. Firewood to be collected, clothes dried out, a search of the shoreline at first light.

* * *

The transformation from raging tempest to dead calm the following morning was a facet of the Galilean weather that all the men had seen before. They moved slowly, their bones stiff and cold from lying on the hard-packed red earth of the cave. At first light they moved out, searching the rugged coastline for those lost. Word was sent back to Capernaum, and more help arrived. Messengers were sent to neighbouring villages that bordered the sea - places like Tiberius and Nain - and from those villages too men were dispatched to search their section of the shoreline.

The men from Capernaum included Simone's father, Jona, his craggy face heavy with the shock of losing his father. He embraced his son tightly, neither man speaking. No words were necessary. It was a family loss. The Rabbi from the village had also arrived, clutching the scrolls of the heavy torah to his thin, gaunt body as though the book weighed no more than a healthy baby boy. He had a somewhat ascetic look, a stiff collar, a trimmed beard, and coal-black eyes that matched his shirt and jacket. He moved among the men, offering words of encouragement to the searchers as they began their grim task. More boats and men arrived from Capernaum.

The sea was kind to the men. It gave up its dead. By mid-day, all lost had been found. Simone approached his grandfather with trepidation. The hair was matted with seaweed that Simone removed. His grandfather's face was as cold as marble, the eyes half-shut and sightless, but the face still bore a hint of that steely determination that had marked the man's life down through the years and which had culminated in his last shouted order to Simone to save the men. Simone gently closed the man's eyes and whispered that eight had been saved.

Burial was demanded straight away. The heat of the land gave them no choice. A spot was chosen on the hilltop, and the bodies of the dead were wrapped in old tarps. They dug deep, on a spot that commanded good views back towards distant Capernaum. Wild animals roamed this rugged landscape - wolves, jackals, and mountain lion. Vultures too.

The bodies were lowered into the graves using a rope pulley system. The Rabbi opened his Torah and read a passage from Genesis. The men stood huddled and listened to the Rabbi's words. They saw him give a nod to fill the graves with soil. And then one by one, they approached the graves and placed stones on the graves. Tradition. Simone approached last; a fossilized stone hidden in his giant hand. His face was stoical, but the tears were close. Very close.

The Rabbi caught his eyes and his lips moved. "Any last words, Simone?" The Rabbi knew of the close bond that had existed between the boy and his grandfather.

Simone looked around the assembled men. "He taught me to fish."

The Rabbi nodded solemnly. It was as good an epitaph as any. He watched as the young man placed his stone.

As the men retreated towards the boats, the Rabbi placed his own stone. Silent prayer ran through his mind. He spoke softly: "Rest peacefully, my brothers."

That night a mourning wail filled the streets of Capernaum. Special prayers were held in the Synagogue.

CHAPTER 3.

20 AD.

The men of the Ciccone clan had always served the Senate of Rome well. Born into Roman aristocracy they were assured of their place in society. They'd fought for Rome, led legions against her enemies, sweated tears for Rome, and even died for her. Cesari Ciccone knew the Senate well. As a young boy, he'd often accompanied his father to the Senate and from an early age he had been immersed in the politics of the assembly. He hungered for the day when he too would be allowed his say in front of the great assembly. Cesari fulfilled his ambitions. He was a powerful man now, but even he felt a sense of powerlessness when he heard his wife Augusta scream out from the bedroom. Childbirth could always be a difficult period. Antioch, in Roman led Syria couldn't boast of the same medical facilities as Rome, but it was where Cesari had been assigned.

The physician attending her was one of the best. He needed to be, because in Roman times the profession was regarded as a necessary evil. The world of medicine could prove beneficial, but physicians were still human and couldn't ward off the more fatal of diseases like smallpox and cholera.

Cesari resumed his relentless pacing. The physician was taking his time. Eventually Cesari heard the crying of a baby, but when the physician didn't emerge from the labour room, he resumed his relentless pacing. His steps were heavy as behest a strong man. He had the chest of a warrior, and strong bear-like arms that swung by his side as he paced the corridor.

After an age, the physician reappeared, wiping his brow, and shaking his bald head. His toga was drenched in perspiration. His gaze flicked to meet Cesari's eyes.

"Well?" Cesari's impatience was rising.

The physician smiled tiredly. "You have a son."

Cesari's grin was as broad as a Roman plain.

"And three girls."

"Three girls?"

"Augusta delivered four babies."

Cesari grinned foolishly. He noticed at once that the grin wasn't mirrored on the face of the physician, and he blurted out: "What's wrong?"

Panic. Sudden panic.

The physician shook his head. "Augusta died. She succumbed to the pain."

A cry of anguish broke Cesari's thick lips.

"Died?"

"I'm sorry, Cesari. There was nothing I could do. She insisted the babies live." The physician's angular face betrayed tiredness, fatigue, sympathy. He wasn't quite ready for Cesari's cold dismissal.

"Get out," Cesari ordered.

"Cesari, I understand your loss...but..."

"Out...out...OUT," Cesari said, his voice rising. He slumped into a chair, his face haggard. Eventually he came to his feet and walking into the bedroom he caressed Augusta's still face. A few slave girls watched him in silence and pity. They had been caring for the four new-borns.

They wondered would he allow the children to live? They knew well the Roman way. A Roman father had the power of life and death over his children.

They saw his gaze flicker to the four new-borns. With bated breaths they waited, but when they saw Cesari lift his son and hold him up to the light they had their answer. They knew for sure when he ordered them to feed the baby girls.

The children would live.

Augusta could rest easy.

* * *

There were rituals surrounding the birth of a new-born.

Some people had adopted the new practice of baptizing babies, although Christianity would not be fully accepted by Rome until the Empress Constantinople accepted the faith in the year 396 AD. Cesari knew that Augusta would have approved bringing the new-borns to the Seer. It was accepted in certain Roman circles that the Seer could help foresee what life had in store for a child.

The Seer was ancient. Nobody knew for sure how old he was. His gnarled hands suggested he had been around for around one hundred and forty years, and his pale blue eyes were sunken in a wrinkled face. Those hands now unwrapped the blanket tied around the baby's form, and the eyes searched for any imperfections on the baby's body.

"What shall he be called?" the Seer asked.

"Luke."

The Seer nodded sagely. "Luke," he repeated slowly to himself. "Lu...ke."

Cesari's face reflected his curiosity. "Will he fight great battles for Rome?"

"No."

"No?"

"His words will resonate through the ages."

"His words?"

"He will be a great scribe," the Seer explained. "He will write a Gospel."

"A Gospel?" Cesari's face was puzzled.

"Yes," the Seer continued. "His life will follow the new path."

"The new path?"

"Christianity...his words will chart Christ's progress here on earth."

"So, he'll be a great writer?"

The Seer laughed, a hearty bellow laughter that shook his skeletal frame. "He'll be a little more than that. A writer, yes. He shall write in common Greek - Noine. But he'll also be a historian, a chronicler of events. He will be one of four. And many will follow the path because of his words."

Cesari rewrapped the blanket around his son's body, his face troubled. He didn't want to believe the Seer. He knew Rome could be harsh in the treatment it lashed out to people who declared themselves Christians. It was a new faith that would develop over the next fifty years in the eastern half of the Roman Empire. He moved to leave the house of the Seer, but the old man wasn't finished. His gnarled hand reached for Cesari's shoulder. It was a comforting touch.

"Do not be troubled, Cesari. I see it in your face. He will reverse the actions of Scarpacco."

Scarpacco!

That monster.

The man who had caused the weeping in Ramellah. In 5 BC. Acting on Herod's orders, Scarpacco had led his Roman cohorts into Ramellah and had proceeded to butcher all the inhabitants under the age of two. Herod's madness.

He remembered that time. A young commander with ten cohorts under his command, Scarpacco had been equal in command. King Herod, whom Cesari recognised as a vain, cunning individual had gone into a rage when one of his advisors had announced three Kings coming into his territory in Galilee unannounced. The advisor said that they had visited a small town called Bethlehem. Rumour had it that they had gone to visit a baby boy who would later be crowned a King.

"A King," Herod had mocked. "There shall be no Kings in my territory unless I make them." His orders had gone out. Cold and merciless. "Seek out this boy and kill him."

His reflections caused him to issue new orders. "No...kill them all. All boys under two to be slaughtered."

Scarpacco had volunteered for the horrendous task. Cesari had been appalled.

Scarpacco had returned to camp the following day, boasting of heroic acts on the battlefield, his sword still bloody from the mayhem wrought.

"Can you see Royal blood on this sword," he had cried in ecstasy.

Cesari had planted his fist deep into the man's stomach and left him retching on the ground. He had stalked away, cursing Scarpacco, cursing Herod, and even cursing Rome.

* * *

The women of the extended Ciccone clan were nothing if not practical women of the day. They had gathered in Augusta's home, and they were holding an impromptu conference on the course of action they would take to help Cesari through his newfound grief. An olive wood fire blazed in the hearth. A hand-woven Turkish rug covered most of the marble floor and a sundial on a nearby table showed the time. Urns and vases of flowers lined the room.

"He'll need a new woman by his side," said Angelina. "Not just for himself, but someone who can care for four babies." Angelina was a woman in her sixties and was the matriarch of the clan. Her face bore the same marked determination that her daughter's Augusta's face had shown in childbirth. She had a steely disposition that brooked or harboured no nonsense. Her grey hair was tied in braids. Roman women prided themselves on appearance and Angelina was no exception.

Angelina's eyes fell on her two youngest daughters - both yet, unmarried. They shifted uncomfortably under her gaze. Rebecca, the eldest of the two, finally met her mother's eyes. She was also the more rebellious of the two.

Kinship and particularly marriage weren't strictly up to individuals' desires. Such matters were normally the reserve of families. As the matriarch, Angelina had a powerful sway, and a powerful voice in such matters.

"Rebecca," she ordered. "Pack your bags. You'll leave tonight."

* * *

The courtship was a slow one.

Cesari mourned his wife for a long time. Rebecca had proved herself more than capable of overseeing the four children for her grieving brother-in-law, the three young girls. But Luke too was a little joy, and because he was the only boy, he got special attention.

Time passed before Cesari saw in Rebecca the makings of a wife. But the day came when he brought her flowers and thanked her for minding his children so well. They would go for walks and talk endlessly about the future and what it might hold for them, and he brought her to plays that enacted the great moments in Roman history.

He could see that Rebecca was a different woman to Augusta. She had given him enough space to grieve, despite having her own grief to contend with. Watching out for the children seemed to have a positive impact on her though, bringing out all the feminine protectiveness that Augusta would surely have supplied had she lived.

Eventually the day came when he saw in Rebecca a possible bright new future and he asked her to marry him. For her part, Rebecca had fallen in love with the quiet-spoken senator, and she quickly acquiesced. Angelina prepared the marriage ceremony with the aplomb of a proud mother-in-law. The marriage was a 'Who's who' of Roman society. An eclectic mix of people got invited to the ceremony. Politicians, scribes, singers, soldiers and poets made up the mix and ensured the wedding proceeded lavishly.

On the morning she was to wed, Rebecca was awoken by a slave girl who brought her bowls of scented water to remove her night mask. Her night mask was a mixture of flour and milk. A more exotic one had been prepared for her wedding night - honey mixed with Libyan narcissus bulbs and crushed antlers from a healthy young stag. Her next task consisted of brushing her teeth and freshening her breath with a sweetener. Her slave girl then prepared her bath, scenting the water and assessing the degree of hotness. As she stepped from the bath, she was treated by an *unctor,* an anointer, who gave her slim body a brisk rubdown and prepared her body for oils. Slipping into a robe, another maidservant called an *ornatrix* arranged her dark Mediterranean hair using combs and pins to highlight her bonnet of curls. Then her complexion was lightened using a white powder, and her wide cheeks and full lips tinted with rouge derived from ochre. Then her eyelids were addressed with a derivative of kohl - an ancient Egyptian cosmetic. Next, she was given her long silk dress, the silk imported from Persia, especially for her wedding. Then she donned her jewellery including a magnificent necklace adorned with gold, mother-of-pearls and deep emeralds.

Finally, her maidservants wished her well and gave her a magnificent bouquet of flowers for her wedding day. A horse drawn carriage waited to bring her to Cesari's side, drawn by four magnificent Arabians.

For his part, Cesari had spent the morning soaking in the public baths, brushing his teeth and shaving the whiskers from his face. His clothing consisted of a magnificent silk toga, and new leather sandals. He smiled as Rebecca arrived.

"You look radiant," he remarked.

She smiled demurely.

He walked her to the altar of the gods and a ceremonial priest proceeded to marry them. The audience clapped their approval, before retiring to banquet rooms for a lavish feast.

That night alone in their quarters, Cesari kissed his new wife. His hands reached for the pins that held her dress together, letting it slip to the marble floor, as she reached beneath his toga. Their hands explored one another, and their breathing became laboured as he led her to the giant four-poster bed. The half-moon visible in the night sky illuminated their bodies as they moved together.

Next morning. They noted with satisfaction that Angelina had made all the arrangements to help care for the children. The happy couple left for a trip to the north. The Alps.

CHAPTER 4.

30 AD.

The *Resurrection.*

Jerusalem had been quiet since the tumultuous events of Friday that had seen the Shaman of Galilee executed on a cross. The Sanhedrin had been busy, and in a meeting with the Roman Praefectus, Pontius Pilate, had demanded that a guard be placed on the tomb of Jesus. Somewhat taken aback by the events of the past few days and left speechless in the wake of the damage wrought on their beautiful temple, they were now going about repairing the damage.

The damage wasn't just physical. They had to cement the image in people's minds that Jesus had been nothing more than a false prophet. They had been disturbed to learn that the Shaman would return from the dead. They denied it as an ugly rumour brought about by followers of the Shaman, and they explored the possibility of arresting all the followers.

They were worried about the teachings of a man known as Petros, and they were also concerned about followers like Stephen. Stephen was a man from Jerusalem, and they couldn't understand how he had been corrupted by these new ideas. The Sanhedrin also worried about changed loyalties within their own ranks, and they tried to bolster their own image in a damage control exercise. All day, Saturday, they had tried to reinforce their belief that they had acted in the best interests of the general populace, but rumours were beginning to circulate around the city that bothered the Sanhedrin.

They had tried to laugh off the rumours, but there was a persistent nature to them that that they couldn't ignore. It was these rumours that had caused them to go to Pontius Pilate and demand a guard be placed on the tomb of Jesus. Pilate himself had laughed at them.

"He'll rise again?" he had scoffed.

Ciaiphas had shook his shoulders. "The people are gullible. They are easily led. We want to quash any hope they have for a supposed miracle...a resurrection?"

"Go away," the Romans had ordered.

Ciaiphas had stood his ground. He chose his next words with care. "This new movement could be very dangerous for Rome."

A threat to Rome.

Words guaranteed to make the Romans sit up and take notice.

The laughter died in the Roman's throats. Threats to Rome were taken very seriously. "If it's that important to you...then a guard will be arranged. Now go!"

* * *

"Why do you seek the living among the dead?"

Mary frowned. Who was this man to bother them on the Sabbath? When they had duties to perform. Oils to administer.

The man's face remained hidden by the first rays of the morning sunshine. Her mood had been dark since Thursday, the day of her son's arrest. It had darkened further on Friday when she had seen her son put to death, and since then she had found herself weeping uncontrollably. She had lost her husband Joseph a few years before and she had thought that bad enough...inconsolable grief...but the loss of a child was something new.

Alien almost. A dreadful feeling of total helplessness, despair, and mind-numbing, life-altering grief.

The scene at the tomb reminded her of something. John had told her of the events. Roman soldiers were sleeping outside the tomb. She was reminded of John's story concerning Jesus in the Garden of Gethsemane when one by one the disciples had fallen asleep. Jesus had admonished them.

"Can you not watch one hour with me?"

She smiled grimly at the memory. It was so like Jesus. The memories of him flooded back. That day long, long ago when he had gone missing in Jerusalem. How she and Joseph had frantically searched for him. When they had found him preaching in the synagogue they had been astounded.

"Why do you search for me when I am at my father's house?"

Spoken through the lips of a boy, but with a manly manner. She had known in that moment that he truly was from God. Earlier memories flooded back...the difficult birth in Bethlehem...the flight to Egypt through the rugged Sinai landscape where they had finally found some refuge...the early days back in Nazareth. Oh...how wonderful those days had been.

She remembered him as an older youth, watching the ways of his earthly father...the skills of cutting wood...using the chisels and tools of the day...bending the wood to the desired shape...planing the wood shavings, sawing through wood and hammering or gluing it all together. She could still smell the wood shavings off their linens. The wood they used could be found on the land - olive wood, walnut. durable oak and Lebanese cedar. The varnishes they had used. All of Nazareth, and the towns beyond had proclaimed their work.

But his real work had been for his heavenly father's kingdom. And for that, all nations would proclaim his work.

She remembered too the glances the girls had given him as he matured. He had danced with many but promised himself to none. In his twenties he had gone off alone on a number of occasions. Sometimes he headed for the dangerous Judean desert, praying silently. Alone in that barren landscape. He was often seen in the company of his cousin - John the Baptist - discussing matters of God. He made frequent trips to his cousin's hometown of Ein Karem. He also made frequent trips to Jerusalem.

Once he was even gone for a few years.

He had kept in touch by letters. Other travellers brought home his letters from places as far away as Turkey, Samaria, and places in the east like Iraq and India. The old silk trails. He travelled widely, taking his own stock of the world his heavenly father had created, seeing at first hand the diverse cultures and customs that had grown up around the peoples of the world.

And then he came home.

To fulfil the prophecy and his mission.

The years of wanderlust were behind him.

As Mary approached the tomb, she saw that something was amiss. The rock had been rolled away. Jesus was gone.

Only the shroud remained.

She suddenly remembered the man on the hilltop. She saw the fearful look on the faces of the soldiers. As she ran back towards that spot, she saw that the man was still there. The hoe was still in his hands. He smiled at her. At that moment, the sun shifted in the sky, and she saw that it was Jesus. Her heart leapt with joy. She moved forward, her hand outstretched.

He moved back slightly, holding the hoe as though it represented a barrier between them.

"Touch me not, for I have not yet ascended to the father!"

She stood still. She could see the wounds on his hands, on his feet, on his head. "Go, and tell my disciples," he said, simply. "Tell them I am coming."

With a final smile, he turned and walked away.

* * *

Seeing Jesus again, made Mary think about her nephew - John the Baptist. He too had spoken of this day. She remembered the time she had made the difficult journey to Ein Karem to visit Elizabeth - the mother of John the Baptist. The year had been 5 BC.

John's mission had begun before that of Jesus. Crowds surged to the river Jordan to hear the words of the Baptist, and to baptize themselves with water. John spoke about the fact that he baptized with water, but that one was coming who would baptize with the Holy Spirit. A day came when Jesus turned up the Jordan to hear his cousin. He approached John. The year was 27 AD.

"It is I who should be baptized by you," declared John. John's disciples looked around. They had never heard him speak like this before. They eyed Jesus truculently.

Jesus answered his cousin. "No...let the prophecy be fulfilled." Jesus bent his head towards John.

John scooped the water up in his hands and poured it over his cousin's head. He heard a heavenly voice.

"This is my beloved son...in whom I have much pride."

"Father, I hear your heavenly voice," John announced, total awe and thick emotion in his voice. Jesus stood again. "His will shall be done."

"His will shall be done." John repeated the words of Jesus.

He watched Jesus walk away. The serenity of the man. The assured nature. The confident stride. His face broke into a smile.

"Master?" His disciples were bothered.

"Follow him," John ordered two of them. "Make sure he comes to no harm."

"And then come back?" they questioned.

John shook his head. "You will not wish to. You must follow him now. As I diminish, he will grow. See where it leads you."

"But Master, our work is here with you."

John frowned. "My work here is finished. It is written."

"Written?"

"By the prophets." he said. "Go now, and don't look back."

They gave him a puzzled look but went and gathered their belongings. They shouldered their belongings, cast another puzzled look at John, and then stepped out onto the path that would bisect the one taken by the Galilean Jesus.

John watched them go and sighed heavily. They were two of his best men.

His work here was done.

Done and dusted.

The sands of time had run out.

He felt the doom marching in.

The heels of Roman soldiers.

The ides of March.

Certain death!

* * *

Saturday. 30 AD.

Although the morning sun alleviated the fears of the previous night, Escobar still couldn't shake the nagging fears that engulfed his being. He thought of going to the temple, and then changed his mind and decided on the markets instead. He needed to buy food. Mediterranean fish, breads, perhaps some fruit. He didn't like abandoning his duties at the temple, particularly as the Passover had begun, but he really wasn't in the mood of meeting with Ciaiphas or any of the others.

The open-air markets and stalls always enlivened him. It was as much a place of talk and chitchat and an open way of mingling and discussing important matters of the day. It was a happy place, with traders bartering and laughing, shouting coarse jokes, telling tall tales, and generally enjoying life. Some of the talk centred on the events of yesterday, but most folk didn't want to discuss death on such a fine morning.

The clothing of the people was colourful and life enriching.

Escobar felt good just being there. He felt alive. The market was full of its usual sounds and smells. A smell of camel hung to the still air, fetid almost. The smell of food was there too. The aroma of spices. All kinds of herbs - cinnamon, hot powders, basil leaves, and the perennial rue.

Barbequed meat mingled with the smell of fresh fruit. Women moved around the various stalls carrying small wicker baskets. The men conglomerated among themselves. Children ran and played everywhere.

Different animals also roamed the markets. Dogs, horses, and donkeys. The markets also sold clothes - fine silks brought in along the old silk trails, togas and linen clothing, leather goods and all the memorabilia associated with ancient living. Lanterns, Greek vases and urns of every size, seeds for planting crops, and even perfumes of every description.

It was at the markets that Escobar first heard talk of a supposed resurrection. Word had also reached the upper echelons of the Sanhedrin council and even at that early moment, unknown to Escobar, some of them had approached the Romans to demand a guard be placed on the tomb of Jesus. Escobar heard the talk but wanted to distance himself from such notions. He felt dismissive. How could any man come back from the dead?

It was laughable.

Still...if any man could do it? Hadn't he brought Lazarus back? Escobar remembered the story but hadn't heard the detail of it.

At the time he'd dismissed it as mere gossip. Superstition.

He moved away from the speculation. He didn't need the events of yesterday darkening his mood. He'd had enough of that last night.

Having returned home, he prepared to go to the temple that afternoon, but he didn't linger. The damage to the temple depressed him. As did the talk that a Roman guard had been placed on the dead man's tomb. He took to his bed early that night and slept much easier.

An excited chatter in the streets awoke him the next morning. He dressed quickly and went out. People stood in small huddles, talking quietly. A man he knew approached him. "Did you hear the news, Escobar?"

"The news?"

"The mother of Jesus went to his tomb this morning with two other women. They went to administer oils."

"So?"

"He was gone."

"Who was gone?"

"Jesus...the Shaman they put to death on Friday. Folk are saying that he rose from the dead."

"How can that be? The Romans had a guard there, didn't they?"

"Your friends in the Sanhedrin are saying that the Romans fell asleep, and that the man's followers came in the night and stole his body away."

"Perhaps they did."

"Do you really believe that?"

"No. I don't." Escobar was thinking of the serenity the man had shown on the cross. The calm acceptance of death, and the way he had relinquished his spirit. The appeal to an unseen God in heaven: "Father...forgive them. They know not what they do."

"You believe He rose?"

Escobar spread his hands in a questioning manner. "If any man could...?". He didn't finish the sentence but left his words hanging in the still fetid air.

***

"Why do you doubt so, Escobar?"

Escobar stared at the man seated across the table from him. His spoon hung in mid-air. Forgotten.

The man had appeared so suddenly that for a moment Escobar thought he had blacked out. How come he hadn't seen the man enter? He realised the stranger was speaking again. "Is it because of Rachel?"

Sudden annoyance bit into Escobar. Who was this stranger to come uninvited to his home and how did he know about Rachel?

The stranger was smiling at him as though sensing his angst. "The room is dark," he announced. "Can you not see my wounds?"

Words failed Escobar.

The man Jesus was sitting opposite him. He could clearly see the marks where the crown of thorns had left their mark on the forehead of the Galilean, the nail wounds in the hands. The table hid his feet.

"Your soup smells good," he said. "May I?"

Escobar nodded his head. He watched in silence as one of the marked hands reached out and picked up a piece of flat-baked bread that he dipped into the soup. "It tastes good too," he announced.

"How can this be?" Escobar croaked.

"There are many with doubts, Escobar. Even amongst my own followers. My brothers, my disciples."

"Why come to me?"

"A favour."

"What?"

"Go to Cephas. Tell him you have seen me. He will believe you. Tell him all sins are forgiven. Tell him of your own role in all of this. It will help to convince him."

"But why do you not condemn me?"

A sad smile appeared on the face of the Galilean. "I come not to condemn. I see the contrition in your heart, Escobar. Men can change. Men like Ciaiphas won't change. They have closed minds. Will you do as I ask?"

"I will."

"Good man!"

Just as suddenly he was gone.

A familiar face appeared on the other side of the table. She reached out a hand for his. It was a human touch.

"Rachel?"

Was he going mad? First the dead Galilean had appeared at his table, and now here was Rachel smiling demurely at him. "I cannot stay," she declared. "I have just a few moments. Our son lives, Escobar."

"Lives?"

"Yes...a beautiful world...beyond this one."

"Where is this world?"

"It's not far," she declared. "A stopped heartbeat away."

"What would you have me do, Rachel?"

"The answer already lies in your heart, Escobar. You must cut all ties to the Sanhedrin, or they will destroy you. You'll destroy yourself by associating with them...listen closely to the words of men like Cephas. They have a steadfast message for the world."

"And what of you, Rachel?"

"I am happy, my husband. I love you. I want to see you on the right path."

"But why can't you stay?"

"It would interfere with your mission."

"My mission?"

"We all have a mission, my husband. Before I go, I want you to see something."

Escobar's eyes dropped. A small boy clung to her wrist, smiling at him. The boy looked so much like him. Escobar felt tears running down his cheeks.

Rachel put her fingers to her lips and used them to touch the tears on her husband's face. "We live, Escobar. Jesus lives. Proclaim Him."

They eased from view, retreating to a world he could not see.

He reached for them.

But they were gone!

* * *

Mary remembered the start of it. 27 AD.

Jesus had gathered his followers.

She knew that things had changed when he returned from the Jordan. She recognised in him a new assurance, a self-belief, a sense that time was spinning events out of her control. She could see that her son Jesus had changed.

Now approaching thirty, he was getting ready for his mission. Followers of John were with him everywhere he went. In Nazareth, he read from the Torah in the synagogue.

Men whispered. "Isn't he that carpenter's son?" Where's he been all these years? What does he mean that today the prophecy has been fulfilled?"

There was an explosion of sound. Men were easy to ire when

their religious sensibility was aroused. "He has blasphemed...on the Holy Book. Stone him...STONE HIM."

Jesus walked away; his head held high.

John's prophets fell in with him. "Master? This is your home...why do they hate you so?"

Jesus explained patiently. "It's not hate. A prophet is never accepted in his own homeland. It is written."

"Written?"

"In the Torah."

*　*　*

Capernaum!

A small fishing village to the north of the Sea of Galilee. Jesus looked down at the place from a hilltop and he knew in his heart that this would be a special place. Here he would gather his followers, preach, set the tone of his mission. Build the stones. The foundation of his church.

The rock he stood on was bedrock - the sturdiest kind. He smiled in contentment. His companions whistled a Galilean tune as they approached the village. The children of the village ran to him, drawn to the man.

Jesus smiled at them, at their inquisitive nature and their questions. A smell of sea air clung to the shoreline, and there were hoarse shouts between the men who fished here. Ropes kept the boats tied to the wooden stanchions that littered the shoreline. A soft breeze brought about a lapping sound of water. The hills surrounding the sea were wild and beautiful and dotted with purple heather. Wildflowers grew everywhere.

It was from this village that he had begun his mission.

*　*　*

30 AD.

A week had passed since the Resurrection.

Somebody was knocking on the door of Escobar's house with a heavy staff. Escobar opened the door and was confronted with the High Priest Ciaiphas and two of his henchmen. Ciaiphas had a long staff in his hand.

"Greetings Escobar," said Ciaiphas. "We haven't seen much of you at the temple. You've been neglecting your duties. Are you ill?"

Escobar allowed the three to enter his home and shook his head. "No. I'm not ill. What are you doing here, Ciaiphas?" he said coldly.

"Escobar, we're going to need your help to round up these so-called Christians," said Ciaiphas, looking around the modest home of the man with disdain. He ignored the cold tones in Escobar's voice.

"No." Escobar's reply was flat and emphatic. And final.

Ciaiphas frowned. "No?" he queried, rolling the word around on his tongue as though it were something distasteful. "Whatever can you mean, my young friend. What's come over you? You've always being dependable before...why change now?"

"We were wrong to put that young man to death," Escobar said.

"The Romans condemned him," said Ciaiphas. "Pontius Pilate. They executed him."

"We all had a hand."

"Including you, Escobar. Including you."

"Don't you think I know that," agreed Escobar, miserably. "But it was your doing, Ciaiphas. You and the council. You persuaded me I was doing the right thing. I know now we were wrong."

"Wrong," Ciaiphas chided. His voice was rising. "How was it wrong? Why this sudden change of heart, Escobar? Are we not all friends here?"

"No...we're not."

The face of the Chief Priest hardened. "If you chose to reject our friendship, Escobar, then the Sanhedrin will be forced to reject you. Do you want that?"

"Doesn't it mean anything to you, Ciaiphas? The storm at his death, the destruction of the temple?"

"Sheer coincidence?" he suggested.

"And what of the Resurrection?"

"The WHAT?"

"His resurrection!"

"Escobar, I'm warning you. Such talk is dangerous. There was no resurrection. That's why we must arrest all of these Christian followers. His disciples came in the night and whisked the body away."

"With a Roman guard on duty?" Escobar mocked.

Ciaiphas shrugged. "They fell asleep. They are human, and prone to human weaknesses."

"No, Ciaiphas. That wasn't what happened. The man arose. That's what he meant that day in the temple when he said: "Destroy this temple and in three days I'll make it rise again. He wasn't talking about the physicality of the actual temple. He was talking about himself."

Ciaiphas looked at his former assistant through narrow eyes. He chose his next words with care. "Those are dangerous words, Escobar. Dangerous ideas. What makes you so sure there was as you put it - a Resurrection?"

"I saw him," Escobar said. "I spoke with him. He ate soup here. He explained things."

Ciaiphas laughed, and his two henchmen looked around half-fearfully. It was an ugly sound, a snort of derision. "You saw him?" he mocked. "He ate SOUP here? What nonsense is this, Escobar?" Ciaiphas gathered himself to go, wrapping his toga tightly around him. "Escobar, you're distraught. Losing Rachel has unhinged something in your mind. You need to see a physician. Last chance...will you help us or not?"

Escobar shook his head. Further explanations would do no good. Jesus had been right. The mind of Ciaiphas was closed.

"Those who aren't with us, Escobar, are against us. Is this what you want?"

Escobar said nothing.

Ciaiphas stood to go. His eyes were angry. "Very well then, my friend. Reject our friendship. We've offered nothing but the hand of friendship. You've chosen to reject that. You're finished with the Sanhedrin council...finished. Do you understand that?"

There was nothing more to say.

Escobar nodded. "You know where the door is."

The face of the high priest as he stormed from the house boded an ill wind for his former cohort and underling.

CHAPTER 5.

20-35 AD.

Luke had grown into a sturdy little boy. His father, Cesari, had been recalled to Rome.

Rome was an exciting place to grow up and learn the ways of the world. It had its dangers of course. The city's makeup of narrow alleyways ensured only carts carrying building materials were allowed unrestricted access. Afoot one had to watch out for the sharp studded Roman soldier's boots, and of the slaves mindless clearing of pedestrians that allowed unfettered access for their masters. Chariots making their way to the games were a constant hazard. But it was still an exciting city to be allowed unfettered access to. Luke loved it. It was so different to Antioch - the place of his birth.

An inquisitive boy, his brown eyes took everything in. He had the same chunky arms of his father, Cesari, which he used with merciless abandon to beat a path through the crowds that always gathered in Rome on the eve of a festival. Even as a mere youngster, Luke liked recording things. He wrote fragments of things on papyrus using a metal pen dipped in octopus' ink. He was looking forward to recording his thoughts on the upcoming festival - the Lupercalia. The Lupercalia always brought out the best in people. They wore their finest togas, with smiles on their faces as they looked forward to a sumptuous feast.

* * *

The Seer was on a visit.

He was insistent on meeting Luke. Luke came forward with some trepidation towards this ancient man. He shook hands gravely with the man, noticing how his little hand was swallowed almost by the gnarled hand of the Seer. The Seer's hand turned the boy's little hand and he nodded sagely as he spotted a trace of octopus ink on the boy's fingers.

"Writing, I see?"

Luke nodded. He saw no reason to evade the truth. He didn't really know who this old man was, but he had been taught to be respectful to his elders.

"Anything interesting?" the Seer asked.

"The Lupercalia."

"Ah...yes," the Seer retorted. There was a slight reproach in his words. "A Roman festival. A pagan festival."

"Just my thoughts," Luke explained, sensing the reproach. His gaze shifted to his father who gave him a reassuring wink. "Where do you come from, Sir?"

The Seer smiled. "It's a long time since anyone asked that. I'm from Palestine and a sect of people known as the Essenes. I knew John the Baptist one time."

"Who's he?" Luke asked.

"He was a great Shaman," the Seer explained. "A great prophet. A cousin to Jesus Christ."

"Wasn't he crucified in Jerusalem?"

The Seer smiled out of those pale blue eyes. "I see your teachers are bringing good knowledge to your ears...we'll talk further of these things during dinner."

Cesari nodded his approval and gave whispered instructions to his head slave.

* * *

Throughout the meal, which consisted of stewed lamb, lentils and beans, the Seer adopted the Hellenistic tradition of using the mealtime as an excuse to teach Luke some truths about Christianity. He spoke with some knowledge about his subject matter, and Luke absorbed the words as readily as the food he placed in his mouth. Like eager boys everywhere, he was full of questions.

The Seer gave him his full attention. He liked children who were full of questions about the world they inhabited, who displayed a bit of intelligence, and who asked smart questions.

Later, when Luke had retired for the night, he turned to Cesari and Rebecca with a grin and said: "That's a smart boy you're raising there."

Rebecca's shrewd eyes sought out the old man. A curious inflexion in her voice as she put a question of her own to the old man: "Cesari tells me that you predicted he would be a great writer?"

"Yes." The Seer's voice was pensive.

"A *Christian* writer?"

"I hear the fear in your voice, Rebecca. However, fear not. He will write a Gospel and what will become known as the Acts of the Apostles."

"And not come under persecution?" Her voice still carried an air of uncertain fear.

The Seer shook his head. "Times will change," he explained. "They always do. Believe me, I know. I've seen many, many changes down through the years. Besides, he'll be quite old when his works are presented to the world. And nobody will bother an old man."

"How can you be so sure?" Her voice had mellowed.

The Seer smiled enigmatically, but he gave no reply. He stood. A tired look had appeared on his features.

Rebecca nodded. She recognised his fatigue. "Cesari will show you to your quarters - goodnight."

***

The Seer was gone by first light.

Nobody was surprised at the manner of his leaving. It was his way. Always a mystical figure, he appeared and disappeared like the desert winds. He would be there if they needed him. He always was.

The only evidence that he had spent the night was a few Roman coins left on the table beside his bed. Alms!

And a book for Luke - the letters within hand-carved in a beautiful scroll in classical Greek. The language of scholars and educated men. The book was bound in burnished leather and felt good to the touch. Luke's eyes sought out the author. It was by the Roman scholar Pliny the Elder and flicking through it he saw that it held passages and writings relating to the Essenes' movement.

Luke held the book as if it were a treasure from heaven.

And indeed, it probably was.

* * *

C.27 A.D.

One of the two men who had left the Baptist to follow in the footsteps of Jesus, had, of course, been Andrew, son of Jona, and brother to Simone. The other man had been John, the son of Zebedee. He was also known as Ioanna.

Although he hadn't been with Simone on the Galilee on the night his grandfather died, the events of that fateful evening had traumatized him. It wasn't just his grandfather, but Samuel, his boyhood friend, and a son of the Rabbi had also drowned, and the two had been as close as brothers.

Andrew changed after that night. He still fished the Galilee with his brother, but he often went missing for prolonged periods of time, and often with no word to anybody.

His behaviour bothered Simone. He felt the concern that was natural between brothers. The day dawned when Simone managed to corner Andrew and ask some pertinent questions.

"Where do you get to Andrew, when you go off by yourself?"

Andrew smiled at his brother. "I follow in the footsteps of John...the Baptist...do you know him?"

"Isn't he a rabble rouser? Always shouting at Herod about that woman he took up with?"

"His brother's wife," Andrew said meaningfully.

"Well, whatever," said Simone angrily. "It's no concern of ours...stop following this Baptist fellow...such associations could be dangerous...who needs enemies as powerful as Herod...I need your help on the Galilee...who is this Baptist anyway? What's his game?"

"Game?"

"Why is he antagonizing Herod in the first place? What business is it of his?"

"He prepares the way, brother."

"The way? What way? For whom?"

"John baptizes with water, but he says one is coming who will baptize with the Holy Spirit."

Simone's eyes narrowed. "Do you really believe that?"

"Yes, brother. I do."

Simone shook his head. "This is about Samuel, isn't it?"

Now it was Andrew's turn to get annoyed. "Don't bring Samuel into this...it's nothing to do with him."

Simone shook his head. There was no talking to his brother. With a deep sigh, he gave his brother a look of dismissal, and turned his attention back to the nets he had been fixing when the conversation had started.

* * *

The man working on the doorway of his house, a single structured dwelling in an elevated position, under the shadow of the Sinai, spotted the visitor from a long way off. The land was dry, arid sand with red blasted rocks everywhere. Lizards leapt from under the rocks, and high overhead vultures circled. The man warned his wife to expect a visitor.

As the traveller got closer, the working man could see that his visitor was young with strong features and carried himself with the look of a man who had travelled far. He was astride a camel, but something told the man that he was not of this land. Further north, perhaps? The land of the Jews.

The stranger pulled up the camel, greeted him, and dismounted with the agility of a mountain cat.

"Shalom," he said. "Greetings and blessings upon this house. My name is Jeshu."

"A welcome to you," said the man of the house, laying aside his tools, and eyeing the stranger. "I'm Ibrahim, and this is my wife, Sarah. Have you come far?"

"Far enough," the stranger replied. "My bones are weary from travelling. I'd like to stay awhile if that's not too burdensome."

"We don't get many visitors. You are most welcome. We're having supper shortly." He watched in approval as the stranger cared for his camel first, and then prepared to wash. The man drew water from the well with an ease that belied his slight frame. He glanced towards the towering mountain and commented: "So that's the Sinai?"

"Mount Sinai," Ibrahim confirmed. "Where the prophet Moses received the ten commandments. You know of these?"

The stranger nodded.

The food was of the land - rabbit with herbs and spices, olives, and a type of sweet potato. There was bread too, that flat baked bread unique to the middle east. Tomatoes too and various salads, again with olives.

"Good food," he commented. He reached into his cloak. "What can I pay you?"

"None of that," they exclaimed together.

The stranger nodded his understanding and sat in thought for a few moments. Then he arose, and without a word, he went outside.

The man gave his wife a quizzical look, and they heard the sound of tools clashing outside. They followed the stranger outside - he had an array of tools spread out on a blanket. Carpenter's tools. A hammer, a chisel, a saw, a planing device, and various nails and fixtures. It took them only seconds to realise that they were watching a master craftsman at work.

The stranger gave them a friendly grin. "You were having some problems with this door when I arrived?" He rubbed the door with the palm of his hand and commented on the grain. "It's good, fine wood," he remarked. "See how the grain runs."

The man of the house nodded and made to protest, but his protests were shrugged off.

Instead he asked a question. "Where did you learn the skills of the carpenter?"

"I had good teachers. My father, Joseph, trained me."

"He taught you well."

"Yes...yes. He did."

"Is he still alive?"

The stranger's face clouded over, and Ibrahim immediately regretted his impulsive question. Jeshu smiled sadly and said simply: "No...I'm afraid he's gone to his eternal reward." The stranger was silent for a few moments. "He was a good man."

"I'm sorry."

"Time helps to heal."

Sarah asked a question of her own. "Did you always live up north?"

"No, I lived in Egypt when I was a boy. I was brought there as a young baby when men were trying to kill me. Soldiers."

The couple exchanged glances, but the woman's shocked voice spoke for them both. "Kill you?"

The stranger smiled sadly.

"But why would men...soldiers...want to kill a baby?"

The stranger smiled. "Babies grow old. They grow up to be leaders of men. Perhaps they had a premonition of that? Herod was a despot anyway."

"I'm afraid we're a simple people. We don't know of such things."

"It's a good way to live."
"You sound like an old man filled with sage advice," the man of the house commented.
The stranger laughed - a deep belly laugh that came from the very depths of his soul. "Do I?" he retorted, still grinning.
Jeshu ran his hand along the wood. "See how it runs- Lebanese cider?"
Ibrahim nodded in agreement. He watched as Jeshu then used his staff to measure both the door and the aperture. He noticed that the Galilean was very precise, measuring it twice, and nodding his head at his findings. He asked Ibrahim to hold the door steady as he planed the ends, shaving wood off with the practiced air of a professional wood carver. He seemed to work with abandon, but Ibrahim noticed he had a keen eye for detail, and that there was a method to the methodical approach he took. Both men then took the door and secured it with fixings. Four hands were better than two, and it wasn't long before the door was swinging freely.
As the evening grew long, they settled in front of a fire, and chatted. Ibrahim had already invited their guest to stay the night, and Sarah was busying herself preparing his room. She used large bundles of straw to make a comfortable dwelling place, added blankets, and it wasn't until her work was done to her complete satisfaction that she joined the menfolk. She brought them tea before settling herself. She listened with her husband as Jeshu told them about his home, and the land he called home. Galilee...it sounded a wonderful place.
Being a woman, she asked a womanly question.
"Are you married?"
Jeshu shook his head.
Ibrahim grinned and commented wryly: "Plenty of time for all that...you're still very young...take my advice and stay the way you are," he said, but Jeshu could tell the words were spoken in jest, with perhaps just a grain of truth. He grinned in understanding as Sarah threw her husband a look of mock exasperation and annoyance. "Men," she muttered to herself.

"It's an earthly thing," he explained. "It would interfere too much with my mission."
"Your mission?" Sarah queried.
He smiled, to take away any sting from his words. He had a straightforward way of speaking, contemplative and compelling, and of holding his audience spellbound and captive. He spoke softly, but there was an iron quality in what he said and how he said it. "We've all been given a mission in life," he explained. "Mine was foreshadowed since the beginning of time and spoken of by the prophets. They spoke of a Messiah that would free the yokes of oppression from the land of Israel. I am *'He'* that would free them."
Ibrahim could see how such words were dangerous, how they could antagonise the wrong ears. In ways, his visitor reminded him of Zealots whom he'd often seen coming through this land. He had been taught as a child to avoid such men. But his visitor was different than the normally hard-headed Zealots he had met before. His message and his words were delivered differently and were consequently more believable. He spoke of peace and love in his words. They were not the words of hate, one normally associated with that of the Zealots, or other warmongers. His words were warm and rich and compassionate. There was no hatred in his tones, nothing but a warm deep understanding of humanity and its many frailties. He spoke with them for many hours until it became time to retire.
They thought he was gone by first light, and they found it a little unusual he hadn't bid them farewell. But as Ibrahim began washing himself from the well outside, he spotted their visitor making his was back down the Sinai. He called to his wife to expect one more for breakfast. As Jeshu drew near, Ibrahim grinned at him, and called out: "You must have been up early. Did you go all the way?"
"To the summit. Some climb."
"Many do it...some go up two thirds of the way by camel or donkeys...but they must finish it afoot."
"A personal pilgrimage. Mind if I wash?"

"Help yourself," Ibrahim indicated. "Sarah is preparing some breakfast."

"Just some tea and dry bread for me," he remarked, as he washed. "Fasting today."

"Is that part of your religion?"

"Our orthodoxy, yes."

They retreated indoors for their meal. After his tea, Jeshu yawned.

Ibrahim commented: "That was a long climb...you might want to catch a few more hours of sleep. You're welcome to stay longer if you wish."

"I'll catch an hour or two if you don't mind, but after that I must be on my way. I've still plenty of travel ahead. There's a caravan ahead of me that I want to try and catch. It's always safer to travel in groups. Too many brigands. I'd like to thank you both for your warm hospitality...perhaps if you ever get to Galilee?"

The question hung there. Ibrahim smiled, and Sarah mirrored it.

"Perhaps," they said in unison.

CHAPTER 6.

28-31 AD.

Much had changed with Simone since that fateful day on the Galilee. Seventeen years had gone by, years in which he had grown and matured and become a man.

His whole outlook on life had changed. Once an easy-going fisherman who relished nothing more than a net full of tilapia, now he worked at filling a different kind of net. A net full of souls gathered for the kingdom of heaven. His life had changed beyond recognition by the teachings of the man known as Jesus. His Master had renamed him Cephas, and the Greeks knew him by another name - Petros. He had known that Jesus was the Son of God as far back as at Caesarea Phillippi, when Jesus had told him he was blessed among men for having declared Jesus, a true Son of God. The last few years hadn't been easy. He'd left his trade, his wife and his children to follow the mission of Jesus. He'd even made peace with his arch-nemesis - the tax collector Matthew - now also an ardent disciple of Jesus.

Fear had engulfed him when Jesus was arrested in Jerusalem. When the cock had crowed three times as foretold by his friend Jesus, he had felt like a betrayer. It was a feeling not dissimilar to what Judas must have felt. Judas had betrayed Jesus with a kiss in the Garden of Gethsemane. In truth, he had betrayed all the apostles, all the disciples, because they had all left something significant to follow the Galilean. Petros knew the high cost of following Jesus, he had paid it, but he wasn't sure that he wanted that cost to include his very life when confronted in Jerusalem.

To this day, he found it hard to understand how he could have denied his friend. He had the feeling that all friendships had to undergo a purification ordeal, although he had his doubts that all such ordeals were a matter of life and death. The best friendships had to be stress-tested. He knew now though that the process had strengthened his resolve and made him a stronger individual. There were times when he could sense the Power of the Holy Spirit. That power was with him every time he spoke in the synagogues. And he spoke frequently.

Following the crucifixion, the Sanhedrin had tried to shut him up. They had him arrested, but the power of the Sanhedrin was no match for God's great will, and he had soon found himself free. The Sanhedrin decided to ignore him, hoping he would go away. Their power was a human power, dangerous only to other humans. As time went by, the word spread.

Stephen had fallen foul of the Sanhedrin though and had been stoned to death when he declared that he could see Jesus seated at the right hand of God. Stephen had become the first Christian martyr, a man unafraid to stand up to human power as manifested by the Sanhedrin, a man who stood for Christian values, and a man not afraid to die for his beliefs. He had also been a leader amongst Christians and following his death they scattered to places like Antioch and Corinth and helped to spread the word further.

Petros had been transfixed by the power of Stephen. The Christian faith so clear in the man had astonished him. Saul, or Paul as he would become known had been present during Stephen's stoning and had suffered a conversion after being struck blind on the road to Damascus. His conversion, and later teachings would help the spread of Christianity well beyond these shores. Petros had being initially cautious of Paul but was soon won over by the man's conviction in his new beliefs.

***

Paul's conversion wasn't an isolated case.

Petros was astounded one day when he heard that a member of the Sanhedrin council wished to speak with him privately. The man who came into his quarters was initially very hesitant, but Petros soon put him at ease. Nevertheless, his opening gambit with the man was harsh.

"You were one of the ones who condemned him?"

"Yes." There was anguish in the man's voice.

"You sided with the High Priest Ciaiphas?"

"Yes." Helpless tones.

"Why come to me?"

Escobar shook his shoulders. "I've heard the elders speak of you. They fear you. They fear what they've done."

"Well may they fear," Petros announced. "However, their fear may be unjustified. My Master forgave them on the cross."

"Yes...I know. I heard."

"You were there?"

"Yes...I was."

Petros was silent, thinking. He himself hadn't been there. He had been hiding in Jerusalem, afraid to venture out. He hadn't wanted to see his friend die. John had told him about the death and the ensuing storm. He remembered the storm - the wind howling, the sudden darkness, the lightning and thunder. He remembered too the cock crowing three times just as his Master had preordained. The sound had pierced his heart. He realised Escobar was speaking again.

"Another man was there that day," Escobar commented. "One of his disciples. With Mary, the mother."

Petros nodded. "That was John."

"The man said from the cross: "John...Behold your mother. Mother...Behold your son!" Escobar sounded reflective. "How is the mother?"

"Mary," Petros said. "She's fine. At the foot of the cross she was heartbroken even though she knew it was God's great plan. She knew from his very birth that Jesus was destined for God's greater glory. That was how he was conceived. A special child. A special boy. Born in a stable in Bethlehem. Visited by three kings in a simple stable. And by shepherds. Guided there by a great star in the heavens. In the night sky."

Escobar listened intently. He hadn't known anything about the birth.

Petros was still speaking. "Mary...met the Risen Jesus. He had told us. But we had forgotten. He had told us he would rise again...on the third day. Can you believe that?"

"Yes...I can believe."

"Many can't." Petros declared. "But I saw him with my own eyes."

"So did I."

Petros looked at Escobar with a renewed gaze. "He came to you?"

Escobar nodded.

"Then truly you are blessed." Petros fell silent. Escobar was equally silent.

Eventually Escobar looked up. A smile appeared on his features. "Is it true he once walked on water?"

Petros smiled in remembrance. "Yes...that's true," he observed, remembering his own terror at the time. A wicked storm had blown up on the Sea of Galilee when the disciples were out fishing. It wasn't the kind of weather to be stuck in a small fishing boat. The men had begun to panic, and since panic was infectious, Petros had got caught up in the moment. Jesus had calmed the men and the waters by walking on water. "He did many remarkable things," he added.

"He saved others from the world of the dead?"

"Yes...he saved Lazarus. And a little girl."

"Lazarus?"

"A friend," Petros explained. "Lazarus had been dead for some days. His body had begun to decay. What he did was amazing."

"How so?"

Petros's voice was reflective. "It was the only time I saw him grieve. He wept. Then he ordered the stone thrust aside and he called out in a loud voice: "Lazarus...come forth."

"And he came?"

"Yes," a tone of incredulity in his voice. Reverence and awe in his voice. Even now with the passing of time. "Still bound in his burial shrouds."

"They're plotting to kill him," Escobar announced.

"Who? Lazarus?"

"Yes...the Sanhedrin learnt what happened to him. They want to silence him."

"We'll warn him," Petros muttered. "But I know him. He won't run. He takes his duties to his family very seriously." He looked at Escobar through hooded eyes. "Why are you telling me this? Why are you risking everything in coming to see me?"

Escobar didn't answer immediately. "Perhaps...I am seeking redemption. Perhaps...by confessing my guilt...my associations...". He didn't finish.

"You'll find peace?" Petros queried, with a smile.

Escobar smiled back. "Something like that," he said.

"May peace be with you, my friend. *Shalom*."

Another silence ensued, broken this time by Petros.

"And what now, Escobar. Do you return to Jerusalem?"

"No." Sudden decision darted into the man's eyes. "There's nothing back there for me."

"Exile?"

"I think so...yes."

"Where will you go?"

"I'm not sure."

"Why not go to Ephesus?"

"In Asia Minor...why there?"

"The man you saw at the foot of the cross with Mary - the mother of Jesus - John. He has established a church there. Tell them your story. I'll write them and tell them you're coming. They'll help you."

"They'd spit in my face, and I wouldn't blame them."

Petros shook his head forcibly. "They'd welcome you with open arms. Trust me...I know them. They're trying to build a church there. They need all the help they can get. Will you consider it?"

Escobar was silent for a long time. He rose to go. "I'll consider it," he announced.

"Good! Then go in peace, brother. And don't delay. Your life may depend on it. Ciaiphas won't easily forget your affront."

* * *

Asia Minor.

The land Escobar had negotiated to reach Ephesus was as old as time itself. He had travelled mostly by camel and occasionally by donkey. He had passed through Antioch in Syria where many Christians practiced. He had traversed much of the route with trader caravans as travelling alone could be dangerous. Brigands and wild animals roamed the land.

He had come through the strange rock formations of Cappadocia, and he had stayed with the people there. They lived in cave houses; the walls painted with decorative art. They had heard about the events that had preceded Escobar's own flight from his homeland, and they asked him questions about that. He could see that there were many believers here. It showed in their artwork. In their simple way of life. In the simple welcome they afforded strangers to their homeland.

He had been sorry to leave Cappadocia.

He liked his first look at Ephesus. A bustling seaport, it was full of people. Palm trees whistled in the sea breezes. He enquired from a few people how he might find the disciple John and they gave him directions. Roman influence governed this town, the streets were wide and paved, the buildings made of white stone, high Romanesque columns. John's church was right in the centre of things.

The sight of John gave him a start. He'd seen this man before. This was the man who'd consoled Jesus' mother Mary at the foot of the cross. Recognition was mutual.

"Petros wrote you of me?" Escobar asked, somewhat fearfully.

John nodded. The disciple looked little different than when Escobar had last seen him. He still had the same lean, gaunt look, almost ascetic appearance. A dark Galilean look, dark eyes. "How is Cephas?" he asked. "Still preaching?"

"Cephas?"

"My Master always called him by that name...his Greek name is Petros."

"His preaching makes him lots of enemies amongst my former cohorts."

"You were with the Sanhedrin?"

"Yes...a member of that council."

John's eyes narrowed. "You didn't speak for Him?"

"No."

John recognised the dismal tone and he waited and watched. A myriad of emotions crossed Escobar's face. John saw all this and still he waited. Eventually he broke his silence. "You had a change of heart?" he queried softly.

"That's putting it mildly," Escobar confirmed. "A tremendous change of heart."

"Cephas gave me the details in a letter," John said. "He works in mysterious ways, doesn't He?"

"Our Lord?"

"Yes. Our Lord."

"Why me?" Escobar asked.

John smiled. "I've asked myself that question many times. Many times."

"And what answer did you receive?"

"Oh...nothing definite." John spread his hands in a questioning manner. "Nothing spoken. Just an internal conviction that I'm doing His will." He paused, before adding: "He must have seen something in your heart."

"When?"

"Perhaps when he lay dying on the cross. You were there, weren't you?"

"You know I was. You saw me there."

"I remember," said John wistfully.

"You were holding His mother."

"Yes. Mary."

"How is she now?"

"Her heartbreak was eased by the Resurrection. She knows her Son lives. She lives a contemplative life in the hills and woods above the town. Would you like to meet her?"

"Very much so, but I'm afraid of what she might say to me."

"Don't be afraid, my friend. She wouldn't want that, and neither would her Son."

"You seem very sure of that?"

"I am." John delivered the reply in a flat emphatic tone that brooked no argument.

* * *

Mary's small, white-washed house was surrounded by very tall trees. Had the trees not being there, the house would have afforded a perfect bird's eye view over Ephesus. John accompanied Escobar to the dwelling. On the way he explained to Escobar the role he had in mind for him within the church.

"You'll bear witness to events. Don't hide your own involvement. Explain to followers you're thinking in linking with the Sanhedrin. They'll respect you more for it. You're not alone in having converted. Just look at Paul. He's now doing sterling work for us in his travels."

"He was struck blind on the road to Damascus, wasn't he?"

"Yes. The Lord struck him blind so that he could see things with a new vision. He was once an implacable enemy."

Escobar turned his mind to the task at hand. "Is Mary expecting us?"

By way of reply, John pointed ahead. "See...she waves at us."

Escobar was growing more nervous as he got nearer. She smiled at them as they approached on donkeys. "Greetings," she said, her voice soft. She had the same dark Galilean look that John and Petros had, and her chiselled features were beautiful, her eyes dark and deep, her hair long and dark. She had a slight frame as though her diet was rudimentary, but her appearance was healthy and life-enriching. Her clothing was simple, a plain white gown with no adornments and sandaled feet. Her gaze was direct and mesmerising and only her eyes hinted at the pain she must have felt in life with the passing of her son.

"Hello Mary," John greeted her, as he and Escobar dismounted and tied up their donkeys. "This is the man Cephas wrote to us about. His name is Escobar."

"Peace be upon you, Escobar."

"And to you."

"You come from Jerusalem?"

"Yes."

"Come into the house both of you. After you wash," she said, pointing to the pails of water near the doorway. That was the custom of the day. A person had to wash before sitting down to a meal. "We have much to discuss."

John grinned at Escobar as they rolled up their sleeves to dip water into their hands. They slapped the water over their faces.

THE SCRIBE

Then they followed the mother of Jesus into the house. "Mary likes visitors from Jerusalem. It gives her a chance to catch up with what's happening."

The interior of the house was simple and prayer-like. Escobar could see that the table was set. Mary motioned them both to sit. In saying a simple grace, she invoked the name of her Son in asking that their meal be blessed. Escobar followed John's lead and bowed his head dutifully.

The meal consisted of feta cheese, cucumbers and tomatoes, herbs and olives, flat bread and fish. Goat's milk and the fruit of the vine were also served. The meal was delicious, tasty.

"So, Escobar," Mary said. "How are things in the Holy City?"

"Word spreads of the new movement created by your son. The Sanhedrin are powerless against the new movement, and under Ciaiphas they are like headless chickens." He talked of Paul and his conversion, and of how Paul intended visiting them soon. Mary listened intently, nodding her head every now and again as something struck a chord, and then she asked a feminine question.

"And the women of Jerusalem? Any contemporary trends?"

It was a question that might have stumped many a man, but not Escobar. He remembered how his wife had often spoken of the fine new silks from Persia and the perfumes from Egypt. He spoke with knowledge about the subject and Mary listened intently, a small smile playing on her lips.

"You speak knowledgeably, Escobar. Your wife taught you well...I take it you are married?"

"I was," admitted Escobar. "Unfortunately, Rachel died in

childbirth a number of years ago. The baby also died."

A look of sympathy crossed Mary's face as she blessed herself. "I'm sorry," she said. " Rachel is such a beautiful name. You're incredibly young to have endured such hardship."

"Youth can have its disadvantages," Escobar asserted, with some bitterness. "The Sanhedrin took full advantage of it."

"The youth are easily led," Mary consoled. "You shouldn't blame yourself."

"But they were responsible for the death of your son."

A film of pain crossed Mary's face. Her eyes sought out John and she motioned her head. He nodded and stood. "I'll go and check the donkeys. Give them some hay." Alone with Escobar, Mary placed a comforting hand on his arm. "Don't blame yourself, Escobar. My son wouldn't want that. He knew what He was doing when he went to Jerusalem. He knew it meant crucifixion and death, and yet he still went. It was his destiny and the reason he came to this earth. He forgave you all from the cross...he asked his father to forgive you."

"His father?"

"Yes...our beloved God in heaven."

"But wasn't your husband Joseph his father?"

Mary shook her head. She explained to Escobar how Jesus had been conceived, and he listened in awe as she outlined the early years in Nazareth and Bethlehem and later Egypt. Mary spoke for a long time and when she had finished, she bowed her head and waited.

Escobar looked at the simple piety of the woman and he heard the truth in her soft-spoken words. When he spoke his voice was full of surprise and reverential awe and he stated something that had been said to her before: "Truly, you are blessed among women."

"Visit again," she urged Escobar as he stood to go. He thanked her for her candour and the meal, and he walked from the house.

John looked at him as he approached. "Well?" he queried.

Escobar shook his head. "A remarkable woman," he enthused. "Truly remarkable."

John smiled. "I told you, you wouldn't be disappointed."

CHAPTER 7.

36-40 AD.

Things were changing in Jerusalem.

Ciaiphas had been ousted from the Sanhedrin, and a new man had taken over the helm. Six years had passed since the crucifixion. The new Christian message was beginning to spread, and strong Christian communities had sprung up at Antioch in Syria, at Ephesus in Asia Minor and in hundreds, if not thousands, of little villages and communities throughout the entire Mediterranean region.

Pontius Pilate too was gone. Recalled to Rome to face charges of corruption. Within a year Tiberius was dead, and the emperor Caligula had taken over, a man every bit as bloody as his predecessor. Caligula made many enemies, and he only lasted four years before he was assassinated. His uncle took up the reins of power - Claudius. Even his mother thought him a fool, but he was shrewd enough to last ten years, until his last wife Agrippina the Younger, the great-grand-daughter of the emperor Augustus, who had been exiled for plotting against Caligula, poisoned him with mushrooms. Her son by another marriage, Nero, then assumed power. But more of him later.
Petros was still in Jerusalem, organising the new church, writing letters to new branches, keeping other apostles up to date on new developments, and generally acting as an overseer to everything that was going on. Since the death of his Master, it was universally accepted that he was the sole heir to Christ's legacy, and his leadership was beyond reproach. As the first of

the apostles to witness the Resurrection, one of his first acts had been to appoint a successor to Judas Iscariot. When members of the Sanhedrin tried to silence his teachings, he replied to them that they must follow God, not man. He had proved to them that he was a man of God by performing public miracles, and many could see the power of the Holy Spirit working within him. Some were afraid of his power, especially when they saw what had happened to Ananias and Sapphira, both struck dead by the Hand of God for deceit, after being denounced and judged by Petros. In his role as leader of the early church, Petros received regular reports and letters about how things were progressing.

He had been pleased to receive a letter from John, outlining the progress Escobar was undergoing, and how he was now one of their stronger advocates in the teachings of the new faith. A true conversion. Not unlike that of Paul, Peter thought.

Paul! Now there was a true conversion, he ruminated. A man who had been present at the stoning of Stephen, and the first martyr to die for the new faith. Paul had held the coats of the executioners. And then, when he was on the road to Damascus, he had been struck blind and had undergone a powerful conversion. After his conversion, he had spent some time in Arabia, before travelling to Jerusalem to meet Petros.

Petros himself had done some missionary work, travelling to the maritime cities of Lydda, Joppa and Caesarea. In Lydda he had cured Eneas of palsy, in Joppa he raised Tabitha from the dead, and following a vision he had received there he converted Cornelius and his relatives, all non jews, to Christianity. Cornelius, a Roman soldier who feareth God was in charge of a century, consisting of one hundred soldiers, and the century was part of a cohort of six hundred men, and was also part of a legion, consisting of six thousand men at full strength.

Returning to Jerusalem, he came in for more criticism from the orthodox Jews. Once again, he was forced to defend his actions.

He seemed to spend his life trying to explain to them that Jesus had been the Messiah long foretold by all the prophets they held so dear. It was no easy sell.

They were equally vitriolic in their argument, stating that Jesus had not fulfilled the messianic prophecies, that he wasn't a descendent of King David in that no man had had a hand in his conception, and that he had not brought about the promised peace.

Petros sighed.

He wondered sometimes if his life would have been easier had he remained a simple fisherman? But then, he admonished himself. He hadn't been the only man to change following their meetings with the Galilean known as Yeshu. Aramaic for Jesus. Hadn't Levi, a notorious tax collector in Galilee, changed his ways, and become a disciple like himself?

He thought back to the days following the crucifixion in Jerusalem. Had it been six years already? It seemed like only yesterday.

He remembered the desolation he'd felt at the death of his friend. He remembered with bitterness the sound of the cock crowing, having denied his friend three times, a sound that had pierced his very heart. He remembered his elation when the Messiah had arisen like Lazarus, and had spent time in their midst, once again.

The Holy Spirit had descended upon them like a dove from heaven and had endowed them with the gift of tongues - a deep-sated knowledge of languages commonly used throughout the ancient world. Sumerian, Egyptian, Greek, Latin, Hebrews, Aramaic, and even the language from the land of Gaul and Hispania.

Following the gift from heaven, the twelve had scattered. Thomas, the doubter, had gone east to Parthia and India. In a strange irony, they had done what the Romans had done with the belongings of Yeshu following the crucifixion, and they had cast lots to decide who would go where. Bartholomew had been chosen to go with Thomas. Bartholomew had then left for Armenia, a country Jude of Cana would also have a hand in. Philip got Greece, Syria and Phrygia. He was joined later by Bartholomew. Simon the Zealot was initially assigned Egypt, but later joined Jude in Armenia and Persia. The brother of Ioanna, James's son of Zebedee, got Jerusalem itself, but he also made it his mission to convert those in Hispania. It was a mixed blessing getting Jerusalem because he would be the first to be martyred for his faith, falling foul of the authorities. Andrew preached in Eastern Europe around the Caspian Sea, in Thrace, in Macedonia, and finally in Greece. Levi went to Ethiopia. James the Less got Egypt. John, or Ioanna as he was known to the Greeks, got Ephesus. Matthias, who had replaced Judas Iscariot, had gone north to Cappadocia, and then on to the coasts around the Caspian Sea, and Aethiopia. Jude of Cana had gone to preach in Mesopotamia, Libya and Persia.

At times they all crisscrossed one another's spiritual paths.

Simone was gratified that the word was being spread in so many places. He remembered Jesus talking about seeds and how they could multiply. It was, he supposed, a bit like tree growth, with branches shooting out in all directions. He thought of the olive trees in the Garden of Gethsemane. What a peaceful haven that had been. A place of prayer and contemplation. Until the night Judas of Iscariot had destroyed everything with his betrayer's kiss.

Everything had changed after that night. Judas himself had been deceived by the Sanhedrin, and when he realised this in the fullness of time, he couldn't live with what he had done, and he put a rope around his own neck.

But Judas hadn't been the only one confused about the mission of the Messiah. Petros himself hadn't understood Jesus's determination to travel to Jerusalem when he knew he would be put to death there. Petros had wanted Jesus to return to Galilee. Hide out among their own.

Galilee had always been a safe haven. The lure of Bethsaida and Capernaum, places where everyone knew everyone else, could be powerful. Perhaps he was just missing the carefree days when he was a simple fisherman.

He realised with sadness that those days were long gone. He had been entrusted with a mission that he had to see through.

Others were dependent on his strength of purpose, and he couldn't be seen to be wavering. As his friend, Jesus, had said: "He was the rock, on which His church would be built."
A rock was sturdy, immovable, resolute, steadfast in purpose. He sighed deeply; life could be hard. He thought of his father Jona, and his grandfather, and how they had taught him and Andrew how to cast the nets. How wonderful and innocent those days, but life had a habit of moving on, time waiting for no man, and things changed. Times changed. Sometimes he wondered where all the years had gone.

* * *

In time, Ibrahim and Sarah felt affluent enough to take Jesus up on his invitation and visit Galilee. Upon arriving they met many people who had known Jesus, but they were shocked when they heard of his fate.
"Put to death?" Sarah had questioned one speaker.
The young woman had nodded her head; her dark Galilean looks serious as she confirmed her words. "Yes. He was crucified by the Romans in Jerusalem, having been condemned by the Sanhedrin." The girl looked at them both before giving them a beautiful smile. "But he rose again," she added.
"Rose again?" questioned Ibrahim, perhaps more sharply than he had intended.
The girl's smile disappeared. Her voice was adamant as she answered Ibrahim. "Yes...he rose again as he said he would. Many of us saw him. After three days he shook off his burial shrouds and rose from the dead. He walked among us again. He ate with us again, and he prayed with us again."
There was no doubting the certainty of her words. Or the simple sincerity.
Ibrahim stood corrected and deeply astonished. Sarah too was struck by the girl's words.
Later, alone with her husband, they spoke about Jesus.
"How ironic?" Sarah commented.

"What?" said her husband absent-mindedly, toying with the food on his plate but not really eating anything, his mind busy.

"Do you remember how he said he had hidden in our homeland when he was a baby?"

"So?"

"He said Roman soldiers had set out to kill him. How ironic that they managed to kill him in the end."

"It's a strange story," Ibrahim admitted. He thought for a moment before asking: "What will we do now, Sarah? Go home?"

"No," she insisted. "I want to see where he lived. How he lived. How the landscapes influenced him. I want to walk in his footsteps. We've seen Galilee. Let's travel south and visit the River Jordan, and maybe Jerusalem."

"I'll see to it," he promised her.

They had travelled south in a caravan - a group of like-minded travellers who wanted to travel in the safety of a group.

There was something magical about the River Jordan - a place where heaven truly met earth. Birdsong was clear in the air - a musical, enchanting quality that hung to the still air, and which decided Sarah and Ibrahim's minds in their sudden decision to convert to the Christian faith and to undergo baptism.

The water from the Jordan changed their whole perspective on life.

It changed them.

CHAPTER 8.

29-33 AD.

Marcus Aurilius was a paid spy.

His jovial, bonhomie face and inquisitive green eyes masked his apparent cunning and intelligence. At face value people tended to trust him, and he was often entrusted with important state documents. He was in fact a document expert. Those who knew him well claimed that the blood of Gaul ran in his veins, and it was a well-known fact that he spoke the French language fluently. His mother had of course been a Gaul woman and she had met his father, a Roman soldier, sent north as part of a legion to take lands. Aurilius had a command of several languages including Latin and Greek, Aramaic and knew many of the dialects used in the Mediterranean regions. For several years now he had been secretly reporting back to Scarpacco on what the Ciccone family were up to. The ironic thing was that he liked Cesari Ciccone and hated Lucicus Scarpacco.

He stood now in the great Assembly Hall and at Scarpacco's bidding he warned the Assembly that a member of their own senate had been conspiring with Christians against Roman rule.

Uproar ensued.

Cesari Ciccone stood to face his accuser.

"Marcus...you betray your master!"

The head of Marcus Aurilius hung in shame, and his eyes couldn't meet the level gaze of Cesari. He fidgeted uneasily on his feet.

Scarpacco laughed. "He was never your man, you old, old fool." It was a harsh, ugly sound.

The Senate consulted with one another, and then a speaker spoke up. "Cesari, these rumours are very troubling. Will you renounce this new faith?"

"No." Cesari was too honourable a man.

"You know what this will mean?"

"I know."

The senators retired. Their faces were grim when they returned to deliver their verdict. They stood one by one.

"Exile."

"Exile," said another.

"Exile."

"Exile."

"Exile."

**

Lucicus Scarpacco wasn't a man bothered by conscience.

A more sensitive man might have had nightmares following the slaying of innocents in Bethlehem, but Scarpacco's dreams were clear. He had joined the Roman army at an early age, enamoured by tales of bloodlust and conquering armies. He had sensed that the Roman army was his destiny and would allow him the level of freedom he liked having. He was a man who liked getting his own way, although like all soldiers he was subject to the disciplines of army life and to the edicts of Rome. All roads led back to Rome.

In the army, Scarpacco found that his lust for blood was satisfied. He enjoyed wielding power over people he perceived as enemies of Rome. Scarpacco loved Rome, although his upbringing had been poor. Originally from a poor slum neighbourhood of Napoli, Scarpacco's family had decided that their fortunes might be better served in Rome and hence they had moved. The young Scarpacco soon found that he didn't miss the brooding presence of Mount Vesuvius and the wretched inhabitants who laboured under her shadow. His mother was from Sicily, a place of secret clans with strong links to Napoli.

In Rome, the fortunes of the Scarpacco family changed for the better. A fortune was made through the games, gambling heavily on horses that the Scarpacco clan had bought. The family knew a lot about horses. By the time he was twenty, Lucicus oversaw several large estates with countless slaves to help run things. It still didn't stop him from wishing to pursue an army career.

He knew that an army career was a good prelude or steppingstone to politics. Wielding political power was his aim in life. Perhaps, the Senate. To hold court in the Forum, that arena of great debate, he longed for such power.

Lucicus masked his somewhat effeminate air by his sheer brutality. He was aware that some men called him Lucy behind his back. Like many powerful men, he had made his fair share of enemies too. The Ciccone clan were implacable enemies, and in particular Cesari. He remembered the day Cesari had humiliated him upon his successful return from Ramellah. The man had left him retching on the floor in front of prominent members of the assembly.

Lucicus had never forgiven the man that. And since that day he had harboured a grudge and he had vowed he would get even with Cesari Ciccone. When he heard from Marcus, an underling he employed to track Cesari, that his nemesis had brought his new-born son to the Seer a savage grin had creased his heavy face. When he heard that Cesari was also planning a Christian baptism for his new children he slammed his heavy fist on the table in triumph.

So, Cesari was now indulging in sorcery.

Many influential thinkers in the assembly regarded the Seer as a sorcerer. They also had a dim view of the new movement known as Christianity.

"Superstitio," they called it.

Scarpacco had important friends in the Assembly, including Sejanus, the head of the Prefecture Guards who the emperor Tiberius trusted like a son. This information was explosive and could prove to be the fuse he needed to destroy the Ciccone family for good. The hint of Sicilian blood that coursed through his veins gave him a moment of satisfaction that he finally had enough information to make an overt move against the Ciccone clan. The knowledge warmed his blood.

He would see the power of the Ciccone clan broken.

* * *

"Leave Rome?"

Rebecca stared at her husband in shock. Her home and

everything she knew was here in Rome. Her mother, other family members, and friends.

"The senators in the Assembly haven't given me any choice, Rebecca. If we stay, I'll be arrested and tried. It could mean being banished to the mines or perhaps even fed to the lions."

Rebecca shuddered. "But you have friends there, Cesari. Powerful allies. Can't they help you?"

"They're hands are tied, Rebecca. They're afraid of this new movement. Scarpacco planned well. He's on very favourable terms with Sejanus."

"Can't you appeal directly to the emperor?"

"Tiberius won't make a move against Sejanus. The man's too powerful. And besides he's away in Capri."

"He should be here in Rome."

"Blame Caesar."

"How do you mean?"

"Ever since Caesar was assassinated, Roman Emperors have always had one eye over their shoulders, suspecting plots against them everywhere. Tiberius is no different. He places too much trust in that astrologer of his."

"So Scarpacco planned this?"

"Yes. And Marcus Aurelius."

"Marcus?"

"He was spying for Scarpacco."

"But Marcus was our friend?" Rebecca sounded disbelieving.

"He pretended to be," Cesari insisted. "It turns out he has been spying for Scarpacco for years."

"I can't believe it."

"It's true, Rebecca."

A long silence ensued as Rebecca struggled to come to terms with the fact that Marcus Aurilius had been a traitor in their midst. She had entrusted her children to him and had treated him as one of the family. When she finally spoke again her voice was resigned and tired. "When do we leave?"

"In a few weeks."

"To go where?" she demanded angrily. Her eyelashes flashed.

"Greece," Cesari declared, aware of his wife's anger but not knowing how best to deflect it. "It's not the worst place we can go to, and it may be good for Luke. It has a hot climate and I've good friends there. I'll deal with Luke if you take care of the girls."

"Greece," she whispered horrified.

"It won't be that bad, Rebecca. Think of the education Luke will have. They value education even greater than us mere Romans."

"It's culturally different in every way."

"Granted," Cesari declared. "But in effective ways, Rebecca. We can do it, my love. I'm tired of the Senate anyway...the political manoeuvring. I want something different for us as a family."

Rebecca had known that affairs of state in Rome were taking a toll on her husband's health. She thought carefully and then asked: "When will we go?"

"As soon as we wind up our affairs here," he said. "The Senate have allowed that. We've enough for a fresh start when we go to Greece. In fact, Roman money goes a long way there. And it will give you time to say farewell to Angelina and the rest of your family. It's not the far side of the world. They can visit as much as they like."

"It's settled then?" she asked.

"It's settled," he agreed.

* * *

It was perhaps one of the great ironies of life that the Santos twins, both born in Toledo in Hispania, an inland town near Madrid, should both find themselves working at sea. They both had the dark olive skin of Spaniards, and both bore features that were nearly identical. Both had long, dark hair, almost jet-black. They were almost the same height, and both had the same-coloured dark eyes. Xia was heavier than his brother, but it was hard muscle honed by years at sea.

Xavier was the more serious of the two, whilst Xia had a more flamboyant air. He was also more stylish in his clothing, often wearing flamboyant Spanish colours, and wide brimmed sombreros.

Xavier was a deep thinker, and Xia was aware that his brother had become a Christian. He prayed and fasted a lot. There were times when Xia couldn't make out his brother.

He wasn't sure where his brother had developed the sudden religious zeal. When he reflected on it though, he realised Xavier had always been the more serious of the two when they had been growing up. In school, he had always applied himself more diligently. It was the same with work when they had gone off to sea together.

Both men normally worked as navigators aboard ship. Each man had an uncanny way of direction finding: watching seabirds in flight, observing currents and things like wind direction, taking soundings, watching the night sky for stars at certain points, and of course keeping close tabs on the movement of the sun. Both also knew about watching for familiar coastal views.

They normally found work together, on the same vessel. They had a system between themselves that masters and captains often agreed to, and which alternated watches both during the day and at night. The system worked well. Both liked the sea, the unending vistas of water, the fresh air. They also liked seeing how other civilisations flourished, an opportunity that arose with each new port that they visited.

There was a feeling that was familiar, but there was also a feeling of the unknown, not knowing what lay around the next headland or bay. Neither brother would have betrayed their way of life for all the spices of the Far East. They had their routine and they both loved their way of life.

Of the two, Xavier probably found it more of a struggle, but he was married and had family responsibilities. Consequently, he tended to take his work more seriously. That was understandable. He was the main breadwinner.

The city of Troas offered the twins one such cultural diversion. Long seen as an important stepping stone between the east and the west, it boasted a major port, a huge population, Roman baths, a *stadion*, a Greek style gymnasium, a theatre, an *odeon*, and numerous markets.

It was also home to a flourishing Christian movement but Xavier joined with them just as a crackdown and purge against them was about to unravel.

Danger lurked.

CHAPTER 9.

25-50 AD.

The Ciccones' settled well into Greek culture and life.

Luke excelled in school and his knowledge of Greek literature and language expanded as he immersed himself in this new culture. Like all young girls of the time, his sisters weren't compelled to attend formal education classes, and they stayed at home under the tutelage of Rebecca and a few slave women learning the homemaking traits that they would need in later life. They were taught weaving, cooking, and other household skills.

Though she missed her mother and sister back in Rome, Rebecca soon found herself enjoying the Greek way of life. It was more laid back than Rome, but in many ways the way of life was even better than she could have found in Italy. The hot sunshine helped, as did the magnificent villa they had set up for themselves on the Greek island of Crete. She helped with their finances by engaging in basket weaving and selling her wares in the open markets. Cesari often had to travel to Athens on business matters and sometimes he brought Luke with him on his travels. He pointed out to his son the Hill of Mars and other famous landmarks that dotted the city.

Luke took copious notes. Even as a boy he was always writing, perfecting the craft that would sustain him in later life. Not everything was recorded in words. Luke also had a fine ability with the arts, and he could draw and paint with astonishing accuracy and eye for colour. Roman architecture fascinated him. Sometimes he used tablets for writing, but he preferred Egyptian papyrus. He made his own ink using a mix of soot from pine smoke and lamp oil and mixed with the gelatine of a donkey hide and musk. He was also capable of making reed pens from bamboo shoots, an art perfected by the ancient Egyptians.

He was a studious type of boy, not given much to frivolity. He liked the fact that he was receiving a good education.

Greece, of course, was renowned in the ancient world as a leading centre of education, philosophical thought, and leading ideas.

* * *

"The words of the Seer have always bothered me," Rebecca announced one night after dinner. Cesari had just returned from one of his business trips, and Rebecca had made him his favourite meal.

He looked up in surprise. "In what way?" he queried.

"The Seer said he would be a great scribe," Rebecca explained. "But I want him to have a proper education. When he's of age, we should send him to university."

"I think that's a great idea," Cesari said. "Where do you have in mind?"

"How about Alexandria Troas?"

"In Asia Minor. Why there?"

"It's renowned for its learning, and especially its medical teaching."

Cesari frowned. "Medical teaching?" No son of mine is going into medicine."

"What do you suggest then, Cesari?"

He shrugged his shoulders. "Politics maybe?" he suggested.

"He has his own mind, my husband."

Cesari's frown deepened. "You've talked to him about this?"

"Yes. I have." Her eyes flashed defiantly at Cesari. "It's what he wants too."

"When did this talk take place?"

"When you were away in Athens."

Cesari was suddenly annoyed with his wife. "Why didn't you wait until I was around?" he asked.

"Because I knew how you would react," she retorted. "You've had no time for physicians ever since Augusta died in childbirth."

That was true! He thought back to that night when he had nearly thrown the physician from the room on the night Augusta died. However, once the initial grief and shock had subsided, he had sought out the physician, and he had thanked the man for his services in delivering four healthy babies. The two men had shaken hands gravely. "I made my peace with that man," he explained lamely.

"Did you," she snapped.

"Yes," he insisted. "We shook on it."

"You're afraid of the world of medicine," she accused. "Ever since that night when my sister died. You've always avoided physicians since then, even when Roman politics were making you feel ill in Rome."

He supposed that was true if he was honest with himself. However, he felt the need to defend his position in the face of his wife's attack. "It's the Roman way," he said.

"But not the Greek way, Cesari. You were right about one thing in Rome. Here they value education. Medical education is the noblest of the professions. It's highly regarded by the Greeks."

He was still unconvinced. "But why medicine?"

"He sees the benefits, Cesari. Have you ever spoken with him about the loss of Augusta?"

"Of course."

"Have you ever asked him how he feels about the events of that night?"

"No. Why should I? He wasn't responsible. What happened, happened."

"Talk to him Cesari. Ask him how he feels about it. Promise me."

Cesari looked at the steely glint in wife's eyes and nodded slowly. "I promise," he said. "I'll talk to him."

* * *

"Your stepmother tells me you want to go into medicine?"

Luke looked up from his book into his father's hard eyed gaze and laid the book down. "Amongst other things," he agreed.

"But why medicine, son?"

"Because I can make a difference."

"It means a lot of schooling," Cesari counselled. "Why is it so important to you to want to make a difference?"

"Because of you, father."

"I don't get you son?"

"Father, you did well in marrying Rebecca. She's been a great stepmother. But myself, my sisters, and even Rebecca can see your pain whenever you talk about my mother."

Was he that obvious? He knew he hadn't meant to be. God, had he hurt Rebecca?

Luke was smiling at him. He saw the anguish that had suddenly appeared in his father's eyes, and he moved to appease the man. "Don't worry," he urged. "You haven't hurt Rebecca. She loved her sister as much as you did. She's honoured you feel as you do even after all this time."

In that instant, Cesari realised his boy was quickly growing up and becoming a man. "I wanted you and the girls to know your mother," he explained.

"We do, father. Through your eyes, through Rebecca's. Through Angelina's when she visits. We feel like we know our mother well."

"That's good, son. But this medicine thing…?"

"It could have helped mother that night."

Cesari blinked. "Helped?"

"A good physician on hand. Good medicine."

"It wasn't like that, son. It was a difficult birth and in the hands of the gods. The man did his best, but..."

"Mother still died."

Cesari nodded sadly.

"Father, you're right in some respects. It can't have been easy to deliver four babies. But there are advances in medicine all the time. New discoveries, new research. It's an exciting field to want to work in. I want to make that difference."

"For your mother?"

"And women like her," Luke explained. "What better way to serve mankind?"

Serve mankind, Cesari thought. He looked anew at his son. He felt pride in his son. He glanced around his son's room as though seeing it for the first time. In some ways, it was like a private library. Books about education, medicine, art, and religion. In fact, books about everything. He realised in that instant that his son was undergoing some kind of learning transformation. He was becoming learned. Hell, he was learned. The boy was always reading, writing, drawing, asking pertinent questions. The Seer had been right. The boy was smart. Intelligent.

He stood to go. Reaching out, he ruffled his son's hair. His mind was suddenly filled with clarity and decision. His words confirmed it.

"Okay, Luke. Medicine it is."

* * *

"Well?" Rebecca queried.

"The boy is growing up fast," Cesari countered.

"Did he explain why he felt called to medicine?"

"He did."

"And?"

"How would you like to go a trip?"

"A trip?"

"Alexandria Troas. If we're going to send our boy to medical school, we'll want to check out the reputation for ourselves."

She squealed in delight. The next minute she was in his arms. "Can we all go?" she asked. "Luke and the girls too."

"Don't see why not," he commented. "It's been a while since were away as a family."

"Oh, Cesari." She snuggled deep into his arms.

* * *

It was in the city of Alexandria Troas that Luke spent his formative years as a young student. He excelled in his studies. Troas was a city of learning. It could boast of several universities and splendid libraries. The city was a liberating place to live. It straddled the cultures of east and west.

He remembered the trip he had taken with his family a number of years ago. They had sailed from Crete. The crossing had been horrendous.

Cesari had found his son on deck. "Seasick, Luke?"

"Yes...horrible feeling."

Cesari grinned grimly. "Sure is."

"Another reason I want to be a physician. To help find cures for sickness like this."

"Let me know when you succeed," Cesari grumbled. "I'm going below to take the weight off my feet. Might help. Goodnight, son."

"Goodnight, father."

* * *

Unlike the night he had entered the world, Luke never found himself challenged to deliver four babies. A challenge of a different sort did present it itself one dark wintry night, however. Awakened from his slumber one night by a frenzied knocking on his door, he stumbled in the dark as he tried to find a lantern.

"Luke," a familiar voice called. "Hurry up. Open up."

Lighting the lantern with some oil, Luke reached for the door and opened it. Four men stood there, holding a fifth man on a makeshift stretcher. He recognised one of the men as a Greek sailor by the name of Santos. The man's face was contorted with fear and anguish. "What's going on, Xia?" Luke growled. "Do you realise what time it is?"

"It's my brother, Xavier," Xia gasped. "Please...you've got to help him. He's dying."

"What happened him?"

"The Romans...they crucified him and left him for dead. We got to him just in time."

"Bring him in, quick," Luke ordered, glancing quickly beyond the four men to the alley beyond. "Are you mad, bringing him here?"

"We'd nowhere else to go," Xia ground out. "Are you going to help him or not?"

"Lay him on the table there." Luke gathered stuff off the table and directed one of the four to hold the lantern high so he could examine the victim. "Nail wounds to the hands and feet," he announced. "Those nails will have to come out."

"Will he live?" another of the men asked.

Luke shrugged. He continued his examination of the man. "I'm not a miracle worker. His breathing is very laboured. Wood splinter wounds...I don't see a puncture wound?"

"A puncture wound?"

"The Romans normally lance a prisoner through the heart if they have to leave a prisoner, or if they want to hurry the execution for some reason or another."

"He hasn't been lanced," another of the men said.

Luke nodded to himself. He needed to act fast. He wanted Xia out of there. The man was too close to his brother. He ordered the sailor to boil some water. That would keep him busy for some time. He ordered another to fetch a forceps from the back of the house. He looked at the man with the lantern and ordered him to keep it high. He pored over the half-comatose man on the table and grunted.

"And me?" The man who had asked whether the victim would live looked askance at the young physician. He was by far the biggest and strongest of the four.

"I'll need you to hold him."

The other man returned with a forceps and retreated as he saw what Luke was about to do. He felt suddenly ill at ease.

Sensing this, Luke looked up and growled: "Get out. Go help Xia." Luke used the forceps to extract the nail from one of the hands. A pain-filled cry burst from the victim's mouth, and he lapsed into unconsciousness.

"He's out cold," his helper observed ruefully.

"Best that way," Luke advised. He worked quickly and methodically now that the victim had passed out. Without any further ado, he removed the nail from the other hand, and then he did the same with the feet. Perspiration was beginning to clog his forehead. He asked his helper to fetch a wet cloth and dab his forehead as he worked.

He tied string around the man's upper arms to stem the bleeding. A hot poker lay in the hearth, and he applied it to the wounds. A grunt came from the man on the table. With the wounds cauterized, Luke applied a cream to the wounds. Then using the boiling water Xia had prepared he cleaned the wounds of any blood remaining and applied dressings. Xia eased back to allow him work.

Luke was examining the man's right arm. It hung askew as though torn from the shoulder socket. Luke caught the gaze of his helper. "This is where I need you to hold him."

"Anything you say, Doc."

Luke jerked the arm back into place with a violent tug. The man on the table grunted again. Luke then tried to remove wood splinters from the victim's body. He cleaned and dressed the wounds. An hour and a half later he stepped back. "I think I need a drink," he exclaimed.

Xia was cautious when he asked: "Will he live, Luke?"

Luke nodded, smiling tiredly. "He'll live. He'll need plenty of rest and sleep. There's a spare room here he can have."

"That's very good of you Luke," Xia stammered. "But if the Romans should catch him here...?"

"He stays," Luke ordered. "I'll need to keep an eye on him. What did he do to the Romans anyway?"

The man who had helped him hold the victim down answered: "Nothing?"

"Nothing?"

"He was practicing his faith. That's all. He's a Christian."

Luke scowled. It was a thing he hated about the Romans. They were a barbarian race and they hated vigorously the new faith of Christianity. They felt it was a slap in the face to their own gods.

* * *

Following the death of Cesari, Luke spent time travelling as a young man.

He grieved for a long time, but new experiences and places eventually conspired to heal his mind. His father had left him a considerable legacy, and this allowed him a level of research he could not have managed otherwise. He travelled extensively, meeting new people in every place that he visited.

Jerusalem filled him with a classic sense of awe.

He walked the streets of the Via Dolorosa, and the sights and sounds in the narrow alleyways, conjured in his mind the image of a man struggling with a heavy cross. In his mind's eye he could almost visualise the scene. The baying crowd stirred to hatred and violence, the jeering and chanting, the taunts of Roman soldiers. As a boy, he'd often seen Roman soldiers marching through the streets of Rome, their heads high, the clunk of their body armour, the sound made as their boots crunched in unified processions. It was a sight that clung to the memory in the same way that seaweed clung to a rocky outcrop along a shoreline. He'd seen their other side too, the rough jests when they were off duty, the coarse jokes and raucous laughter when drinking beer and wine.

He came to the spot where Pilate had announced "Ecce Homo." Behold the Man.

He paused here, a silent prayer running through his mind. The different incidents that had happened crossed his consciousness: Jesus falling, Veronica wiping his face, the meeting with His mother, the help given by a good Samaritan.

He resumed his walk, relentlessly reliving the stations of pain. Mount Calvary wasn't what he expected. He'd half-expected a high mountain overlooking the city, but the site of crucifixion was just another part of the city and was being built upon even as he looked.

Having walked through most of the Via Dolorosa he eventually found the man known as Petros preaching in a small church. He took a seat near the back of the church and watched as the apostle gave a talk about scriptures. He could see that this was the man he'd been warned to seek out by the Seer.

He noted the big brawny arms of the former fisherman, the big frame that dwarfed the altar upon which he stood, the level eyes and calm stentorian voice. The man spoke with authority, and the scripture he was speaking about came alive for his audience who were listening intently. This man didn't need a book or the Torah. His words came direct from the heart. They were simple words spoken with true depth. Luke sat enthralled.

When the service had ended, the listeners filed out. Luke remained, and Petros saw him. He approached the young scribe, his hand outstretched.

"We haven't met," he said. "My name is Petros. A simple fisherman from Galilee. Did you like the service?"

The fisherman's grip was firm and strong.

Luke winced and replied: "Very much so." He explained how he'd been asked to seek Petros out.

Petros eyed Luke. "You're a scribe?"

"A writer, yes."

"And you intend writing a story about Christianity?"

"A gospel," agreed Luke. "Like the work of Matthaios."

"That's some undertaking."

"I've been preparing for it all of my life."

"We must talk of this further," Petros said. "It's getting late. Will you join myself and my wife for dinner tonight?"

"Delighted to," Luke smiled.

* * *

The dinner that night included tilapia - the fish Petros used to cast his nets out for in the Sea of Galilee.

The wife of Petros still lived there, but she was in Jerusalem to visit her husband and to celebrate Passover. A simple pious woman, she had understood her husband's desire to follow Jesus, a fellow Galilean that she had known also. She remembered the day when Jesus had called to their Capernaum home and had cured her mother of a debilitating fever. It was then when she fully understood who Jesus was.

They sat down to enjoy the meal, and Petros invited their guest to say a few words of thanksgiving.
"Bless this bounty of the sea, Lord. Bless this exalted company and enlighten us all in your ways," Luke intoned, bowing his head. "Amen."
"Amen," said Peter and his wife in unison.
The meal was simple and delicious. Throughout Luke spoke of his plans for a new gospel.
It sounded captivating. Timeless. Enchanting. Magical.

CHAPTER 10.

51 AD.

It was in the northern city of Alexandria Troas that Luke first met Paul. Over the years he had heard things about Paul, some not to his liking, because rumour had it that in his early years Paul had a strong hand in persecuting Christians. But then something had happened to change all of that.

Paul had undergone a transformation so astonishing that he was now regarded as one of the strongest advocates of the new faith. Luke had followed his journeys with mounting interest and no little amount of pique. He wondered what made men like Paul tick.

He hadn't prepared himself for the physical abnormality apparent in the man. The shoulders were stooped as though he carried a huge burden, but the eyes burned with a zeal that seemed otherworldly. An ascetic look pervaded the missionary, skeletal almost, and he retained the beard so beloved of orthodox Jews. His bony hand grasped Luke's in a firm handshake. His voice was strong, like his handshake. "I've heard you are a man of God, scribe," he greeted. "Peace be with you."

"And to you," Luke replied. "You're from Tarsus?"

"Cilicia," Paul confirmed. "These are my companions."

He introduced a man called Timothy and Silas. Luke greeted them and shook hands with the two men. He suggested they talk over a meal.

The three missionaries agreed, and they retired to a tavern that served food. Luke questioned Paul closely about his mission, taking scrupulous notes all the time, and showing by his questions that he was already a man of some considerable knowledge himself in Judean matters. Paul was impressed and remarked on that fact to the young scribe.

"You've studied well," he observed.

Luke allowed himself a little smile. "I've studied the work of Mark," he explained. He told them something of his childhood and mentioned the Seer who had given him a book when he was young on the Essenes' movement. "I think that book awakened in me a lifelong interest and passion about Judea and its people."

"The Seer," Paul remarked. "I've met him. He reminds me of John in Ephesus."

"How so?"

"He seems to live for ever. Nobody knows his age, except for the fact that he's ancient. John is like that. Some of his closest disciples claim he'll never die. They said Jesus himself promised that."

"Do you believe that?"

Paul shook his head. "Not really. They'll both die someday. It's just that they have been honoured and privileged to live exceptionally long lives. It's rare in these times for many men to reach beyond fifty, so the fact that they're both still around just goes to prove that God has a mighty plan for them. Perhaps you're the reason?"

"Me?"

A faraway look entered Paul's eyes. He looked preoccupied, like he was staring into a dark abyss, a future only he could see. His voice sounded far away when he spoke: "Yes...you," he explained. "The work of the gospel writers will reach deep into the future. It will be a path for men to follow. A path to true salvation for all of humankind."

"That kind of thinking gets you into some trouble," Luke commented, with a grin, showing he had a strange insight into the way humanity viewed the bald missionary in front of him.

Paul smiled sadly. "You mean the orthodox Jews?"

"Yes...mainly them."

Timothy decided to answer for Paul, and beside him Silas nodded his head in agreement. "They've always regarded Paul with suspicion. They believe that the message of salvation was for them only, and they refuse to countenance the fact that uncircumcised gentiles and pagans, are equally worthy of redemption."

"Because of God's promise to Moses and earlier prophets?"

Paul looked up from his reverie. "That's right," he exclaimed. "They see themselves as God's chosen people, but they are ignoring the message that his Son brought."

"Will that ever change?" Luke asked.

"How long is a piece of string?" Paul queried. "Who knows? Perhaps someday...?" He glanced out at the gathering darkness. "The night draws to a close. We'll talk further of these things tomorrow."

***

"Have you met Ioanna?" Paul's level gaze met the eyes of Luke.

Luke shook his head. "Not yet," he announced.

Paul nodded to himself. "You must go to Ephesus and meet our people there," he urged. " Ioanna leads the church there."

"He knew Jesus personally?"

"Yes...he did. The mother of Jesus also lives there. And so too does Escobar."

"Who's Escobar?"

"He was with the Sanhedrin when Jesus was denounced and crucified in Jerusalem. Like John and Mary, he was an eyewitness. After the crucifixion he underwent a conversion not dissimilar to my own, and he now believes in Christianity. They practice the new faith there. You must talk with them. They have a first-hand knowledge of the events."

All too well, Luke knew the value that could be placed on actual experience. Time could play havoc with the memory, and stories became distorted over time. People heard one thing and reported another. As a scribe he had a duty to go directly to the source of the story and speak with the people who had been directly involved in the events. Nothing less would do. So, he agreed to Paul's suggestion and announced his intention to travel to Ephesus.

***

Several months passed before Luke fulfilled his promise to Paul to visit Ephesus. Travel was difficult in biblical times. It took time to reach unfamiliar places. People travelled by foot, but in most cases, animals were used - horses, donkeys, and camels. On the seas, boats travelled on sail and oar power, which was reliant on favourable winds and weather conditions. All types of travel were hazardous, and travellers had to ensure they were properly equipped before undertaking journeys. Water always had to be considered, because to be without water in a dry climate, especially in desert areas, meant death. Most people travelling long distances joined caravans. It was simple sense. They had a better chance of reaching their destination when they pulled together with like-minded travelling folk.

The heat of the land could never be discounted, but neither could the extreme cold that penetrated the deepest bones at night. In embarking on a long journey, the seasons needed to be borne in mind. Other considerations included food and how best to preserve it and make it last, food and water for the animals, medicines for those who fell ill, the ability to have proper tools along for any emergencies that may arise, and the necessary condiments to make fires.

A caravan often had a leader who ensured all these things were met, but the onus and responsibility lay on everyone's shoulders. Shirkers weren't tolerated. Everyone had to pull their weight. A weak link in a caravan could mean the whole party losing their objective, and if that happened disaster usually followed. So, leaders were usually picked who had a strong personality, and who could help lead by example. The leader of a caravan needed to be tough and brave, tenacious, generous with his time, but also a man who cared for the people under his control. In some ways he needed to be all things to all people.

It was a tall order.

The caravans also ensured that goods could get around. Many of the caravans followed the old silk trails, trails that had proven themselves before, the knowledge of each handed down through the generations to make travel as safe as possible. Experience was a useful barometer, and it was a foolish leader who didn't take previous expeditions into account or who tried to cut a new path through unknown territory. Navigation was often aided by the stars, and maps were regularly consulted.

Paul and his companions had decided they would go with Luke. At the end of each missionary journey, Paul often had the need to check back with church leaders on how best to proceed next. As head of the church, John needed to be consulted. Although Jesus had entrusted Petros with this title, the people looked to guidance from one who lived amongst them, and they saw Ioanna as their leader. Paul also saw Ioanna in this light.

* * *

Escobar had settled well into life at Ephesus.

He made it a point to visit Mary in her home every week, and she continued to counsel and advise him. Sometimes he went to visit her with John, and other times he travelled alone. He was always made welcome.

John had given him sound advice when he first arrived. He didn't try and cover up his own involvement, through the Sanhedrin, in the death of Jesus. Contrary to his fears, he found that the people of Ephesus accepted him as he was. Some were interested in the work of the Sanhedrin council, and they asked him questions of that. Escobar answered them as best he could.

In many ways he did bear witness to what had happened that fateful day in Jerusalem. There were very few who had witnessed the events as he had. The people here didn't need miracles to believe or wonders from the heavens. They believed and that was that. Many passed the story to their children, and in that way the story passed from generation to generation. It wasn't just the work of the apostles that caused the word to spread, but the simple piety of the people and their ability to pass knowledge and wisdom to their offspring. There was something almost magical, and mystical, that appealed to the children whenever they heard stories of Jesus. They were equally enthralled by stories from the Old Testament and characters like the prophets, Moses, Samson and Deliah appealed to their young senses.

He had found work teaching young school children. The work was spiritually uplifting and rewarding. He wondered what Rachel would have made of it all, and then he smiled in fond remembrance. She would have liked his new choices. Of that, he had no doubt.

John, or Ioanna as he was known had pulled him aside one day for a serious talk. He opened the conversation without preamble. "You made bad enemies back in Jerusalem with leading members of the Sanhedrin?"

"What have you heard, Ioanna?" He could never remember seeing the man look so serious.

"Ciaiphas sent two men out after you...they were asking plenty of questions...who you left Jerusalem with...and they followed your trail north as far as Cappadocia. They hit a brick wall there. Our people wouldn't tell them anything."

"Two men?" Escobar was curious.

"Sicarii," Ioanna said meaningfully.

Religious assassins, Escobar thought. He was thoughtful.

Ioanna was smiling. "You made many friends amongst our flock in Cappadocia. It's our understanding that when they couldn't elicit further information as to your whereabouts, they gave up and turned back.

"Thank God for that," Escobar said.

"Yes," Ioanna agreed, still smiling. "I thought you should know anyway."

CHAPTER 11.

47 AD.

Luke had spent several months in Ephesus, living and learning with the thriving Christian community there. Paul had introduced him to Ioanna, and it was through Ioanna, or John, that Luke met Mary, the mother of Jesus. He also met and talked with Escobar who was able to supply a different viewpoint of the crucifixion, including an insight into the thinking of men like Ciaiphas and Annas. Eventually though, he knew he'd have to return to Jerusalem, and when Ioanna heard of his plans he came to see him.

You're going to the Holy City of Jerusalem?"

Luke nodded. "I have business there."

"You could do us a big favour," Ioanna said. "Mary wants to go back."

Luke frowned. "Would she be able for the trip? I thought she'd made her home here...it's a fairly arduous trip."

Ioanna sighed. "I've explained that to her. But she's insistent on seeing the Holy City again before she dies."

"Dies?" Luke was shocked.

"She's been warned in a dream that her time is near. She says it's the same angel that appeared to her when she was a young girl.

Gabriel. Seemingly he's told her that she must return."

"I wonder do these angels understand the hardships we labour under?" Luke growled in exasperation.

Ioanna grinned at him. "That thought has struck me too."

Luke thought of the simple face of Mary, the expectant beam on her countenance as she welcomed fellow Christians, and he knew he wasn't the type of man to disappoint that lady. If she wanted to go to Jerusalem, then Luke would gladly bring her. He said as much to Ioanna.

Ioanna clapped him on the shoulder. "Good man. I'll let her know."

* * *

It was the time of goodbyes.

Mary had tears in her eyes as she looked at her good friends prior to leaving Ephesus. She had already said goodbye to Escobar, reminding the man to keep strong his faith. Many families had come along to see her off. She knew them all, and their children's names. Many gave her little gifts.

They gave her time alone with Ioanna. They knew a special relationship existed there. A mother-son relationship. Ioanna looked at her with concern in his eyes. "You're sure?" he asked.

"Leave it alone now, Ioanna," she said. "I'm sure. My chariot awaits in Jerusalem."

"Your chariot?"

"It's what Gabriel showed me in the dream."

"Who knows the way of the Lord?" he commented.

"Indeed!" she exclaimed. A brief smile lit up her features. "You've done an excellent job here, Ioanna. My Son is proud of you."

"Thanks, mother." It was one of the few times he'd used that expression. His thoughts had reverted to the scene of the crucifixion. "Ioanna...Behold your mother. Mother...Behold your son."

Mary remembered the scene every bit as well as Ioanna. "Goodbye, my son." Her voice was breaking. She fought to hold back her tears and smiled sadly. "You'll keep up the excellent work?"

"Do you really have to ask?"

"No."

They embraced like good friends. Stepping back, he placed his hands on her shoulders and looked into her eyes. He kissed her on both cheeks. Smiling at her, he said: "You're safe with Luke. He'll look out for you."

"Peace be with you, Ioanna!"

"And to you, Mary. I'll pray for you."

He could not in the end meet her gaze for fear of revealing the tears that lurked in his eyes. Mary too was sad. This was the man who'd brought her north to Ephesus after her Son had died. He'd cared for her like he really was her son. He had visited her regularly, had brought her to his church every Sabbath, and had even made sure she was well equipped with logs during the winter months. She had one final gift for him. She handed him a cross, beautifully carved from olive wood. "I made it myself," she explained, as she thrust it into his hands.

He looked at it in awe. "It must have taken you months."

"Months," she agreed with a smile. "But I learnt from the best carpenters in the business. My husband Joseph, and my Son Jeshu."

He watched her walk away towards where Luke waited. He cradled the cross in his hands. Surprise and wonder were in his eyes. He remembered the time when he had first brought Escobar to see her and the comments he had made after their first meeting. "A truly remarkable woman."

"Truly," he thought. "A very remarkable woman."

Blessed!

* * *

Luke's business back in Jerusalem included a meeting with the Evangelist Mark. It was good to compare notes with other scribes. Much of Mark's work consisted of anecdotes provided by Petros - a direct witness to the events and a source that couldn't be overlooked.
Luke spoke to as many witnesses as he could find as to the events that had happened in Jerusalem.
His writings indicated a growing maturity and innate knowledge of the facts and he put more of a personal spin on many of the stories. His anecdotes were different to that of other gospel scribes and had a more human touch.
He liked Jerusalem. It was a city of contrasts. Bordered on one side by the Mount of Olives, the city probably had more places associated with the life of Jesus than any other place, with the possible exception of Galilee. It had been captured by King David from the Jebusites during the 4th millennium BCE. David's son, King Solomon, commissioned the building of the first temple. The Jews laid claim to the city due to their descendancy from the

ancient Israelite Kingdom of Judea.

Luke liked going to the Garden of Gethsemane with its gnarled olive tree trunks, a place he knew Jesus had liked, for moments of reflection. The place allowed him to think.

It wasn't a huge garden, but its square shape at the foot of the Mount of Olives allowed for wonderful views out over the city and was the perfect place for meditation and prayer. He had written to Ioanna in Ephesus explaining that Mary was now back in her homeland and that they had arrived safely.

He was glad he had brought Mary with him on the trip. During the long journey she had filled him in with elements of the life of her son that weren't covered by other gospel scribes.

***

The Seer also came to see Luke when he was in Jerusalem. Luke welcomed him warmly, remembering the beautiful, scrolled book he had received as a child.

Nobody knew the whys and wherefores of the mystic known as the Seer. He was a nomadic type of figure, a tall, thin man of indeterminate age with an ascetic appearance and some people were afraid of him. They said he reminded them of the grim reaper because he appeared to them in dreams, sometimes carrying a giant scythe and at other times a sword of vengeance. Whatever the truth of that, there were others who were comfortable with his presence, almost as though he were a giant angel sent by God to guide and protect.

Some thought he hailed from the people known as the Essenes and others thought he was of the Tectosages in Galatia because it was known he had dwelled there for a long time. It was obvious that he had power working within and around him. One of his more prominent features was his skull which was very pronounced, and it was also known that he could go without food for what seemed an extraordinary amount of time, almost as though he were living on a higher plane than mere mortals and that plane could sustain him. He lived a strange life.

He was very much a loner and didn't seem to have a woman, or indeed any family whatsoever. He never talked of parents or siblings. It was as though he had come into life on a wing and a prayer, appearing from place to place like a wisp of wind, and disappearing like a gust of wind. He often carried a long staff especially when he was walking, and he reminded some people of Moses who had led his people out of bondage in Egypt incurring the wrath of the Pharaoh but delivering them nonetheless to the Promised Land.
He was known throughout the entire Roman Empire as the Seer. They knew he had travelled far and wide because he often talked of travels north to strange places like Gaul, Britannia, and even Hibernia. He spoke of tribes and clans living that far north and of how they endured through miserable weather conditions, carving out an existence from the green land and the forests and the sea.
There were some who said that when he arrived at a place they seemed to hear the swishing of wings, although nothing like that was visible to the mortal eye. There were others who claimed that he seemed to tower over them in their presence as though he were some Goliath about to face the slingshot of the mighty King David. Others thought he had the wisdom of King Solomon and sought him out seeking enlightenment. A few even thought he was linked in some way to King Midas, but they probably thought that because both had links to Phrygia.
The Seer looked at Luke with his wise and age-old eyes, pleased at how the boy had grown into a fine young man. He put a question to Luke.
"Have I started yet?" Luke repeated. "My gospel? I'm working on it. Researching, talking to witnesses, it takes a lot of time."
"It's a massive undertaking," the Seer admitted. His eyes took on a faraway look as though he could see deep into the future. "But mark my words, your words will resonate through the ages and will create much happiness."
"Scary?" Luke's voice was quiet.
"Quite!"

"Why happiness?"

The Seer's eyes took on a distant look again. "Your gospel will be different and will have more immediacy. Your description of the nativity scene will bring about a happy feast. It will become known as Christmas and it will be very joyous, particularly for children."

"Like heaven?"

The Seer nodded enthusiastically. "Exactly, like that," he promised. "People will be enthusiastic and enthralled by a story of a baby King born to a virgin mother of Galilee and her husband Joseph, a simple carpenter. They will see the weight of the event from the importance shown by the three wise men: and by others of important standing in the community. And lastly, they will empathize with the death of the man, and they will rejoice with his Resurrection."

CHAPTER 12.

48 AD.

Ioanna opened the letter from Luke with some trepidation. Letters arrived through the *'cursus publicus'* or the public way, either overland by horseback or by sea. The *'cursus publicus'* had been established by Augustus and was a state-run postal system used to transport letters, documents and tax revenues.

It was as though he sensed that it contained sad news. He was right. Certain passages caught his eye immediately: "news that it grieved him to tell…a peaceful end…Mary had passed away." He sighed and his eyes fell on the cross he had been given by Mary some six months before. He returned to the beginning of the letter and read Luke's letter from the start. As he continued to read, his eyes widened in astonishment at Luke's tale. According to the young scribe, Mary had departed this world in a chariot. One minute there, the next gone.

Ioanna laid the letter aside for a moment and pondered. Hadn't she said that was how it would happen? He had thought she was jesting.

There had been no long deathbed scenes, no grief, and no sickness. It was as though the walls of the house they had been in just dissolved away and suddenly the chariot was there. The gates of heaven had opened, and Mary had boarded the chariot waving at them. It was like she'd simply stepped onto a sailing boat.

Luke himself had been taken aback by the event.

It showed in his writings.

Ioanna put the letter away. It would make a good homily at his next service.

He reached for the cross and left his house. He walked slowly. There were times he could feel his age catching up with him. He no longer had the ease of use with his limbs he'd enjoyed as a young man. Though he came from a family of fishermen, John himself was a learned man. He had been sent to a university as a young man to learn the ways of the world.

Arriving at his church, he entered and walked the full length of the church he had built here. He had never realized before how big it was.

Near the altar he fell to his knees.

His hands were clasped in a steeple.

He prayed.

Fervently.

***

In Jerusalem, Luke was examining the icons he had painted of Mary.

They were a good likeness, but he felt something was lacking. He was, he knew, a chronicler of events, and he decided it might be a worthwhile exercise to start committing events into writing. He had told Paul that he intended writing a gospel, and he had conducted interviews with Mary, Ioanna and Escobar in Ephesus. He had been meticulous in his note taking.

He had been impressed that Ioanna or John also had plans to commit a gospel to paper. It made sense, as Ioanna, had a first-hand knowledge of the events. He had walked with Jesus.

But Luke also had a talent for painting. He used sketches too in his work as a physician, drawing body parts, and building a chart in his brain of various body parts that were sensitive to the touch of the forceps.

He knew how to add colour and shadows to his work, and how to give the eyes the right luminosity and to make it appear to the casual observer that they were alive. It was all about detail and light.

He worked throughout the morning on his icons, observing from different angles and adjusting the lighting conditions, a tiny brush in his hand as he made slight adjustments. He became so engrossed in his work that he lost track of time. He only realised the time when the hunger pangs set in.

Time was measured in different ways.

Sometimes it was as simple as looking at the sky. Sundials and the use of shadows could provide an accurate barometer of time, and hourglasses with shifting sands were also used. Sexagesimal devices and water propelled clocks were also utilised. The ancient Sumerians had discovered in the third millennium BC that using a base of sixty, sexagesimal numbers and fractions were made infinitely easier because sixty was the smallest number that was divisible from the numbers one through to six. It explained why there were sixty minutes in an hour, or six ten-minute segments, or twelve five-minute segments and so on.

Luke was using a sundial which worked best in clear weather and as the day outside was hot and sunny, it was perfect for timekeeping. He had been working for five hours and was so engrossed that he'd lost track of time. One of the vagaries about living alone was that he had to prepare his own food, but he realised he'd rather go out. He'd drawn water from the well earlier and he now used it to clean the paint from his hands and to splash some cold water onto his face. He then left his dwelling and walked to a local inn where he ordered a pitcher of goat's

milk and a meal that consisted of swordfish, greens, tomatoes, olives, cheese and baked flatbread. He observed the world around him as he ate and conversed with people that he knew.
They knew too when to leave him in peace; he was after all their physician, neighbour, and friend.
Luke sighed contentedly. It was good to know one's place in the world. His mind turned to a problem that had vexed his work from the beginning.

***

Q.
One of the main sources of the events culminating in the crucifixion in Jerusalem of Jesus was the source known as Q. His or her proper name had been lost in the mists of time, and although Luke made strenuous efforts to discover this name, his investigations proved fruitless. It was frustrating, to say the least. The Q source had informed the work of Mark and forced Luke to examine again the life of Jesus and in particular his followers. Could one of the twelve apostles be the mysterious figure known as Q? It was a tricky question to answer because they had all scattered like seeds from a mustard tree. He looked for those who might have had a degree of education and a good grasp of language but many of the apostles had been simple men - fishermen or other trades that required hard graft. He looked hard at the life of Judas, but then he ruled him out. Judas couldn't have been the Q source, even if he had been an educated man.
He looked at the people who had surrounded Jesus, and mulled over the possibility of Joseph of Arimathea.
Joseph had gone to Pilate after the crucifixion and had asked for the body of Jesus, so that it may be interred in a tomb that he had intended for his own use without delay for the Sabbath was fast approaching, but try as he might Luke could see no evidence that he was the 'Q' source. Luke then examined another close confidante of Jesus, a man by the name of Nicodemus. He

was a possible contender because it was known he had written an apocryphal gospel derived from an earlier Hebrew work - a work that was known as the Acts of Pilate. But once again, Luke could find no definitive proof that Nicodemus was the source he looked for, and he shook his head in frustration.

***

If John the Baptist had paved the way for Jesus, then the seventy disciples chosen by Jesus helped to pave the way of the twelve apostles as they went about their evangelization missions. They included Jacob, the brother of Jesus and the first bishop of Jerusalem who was succeeded by Cleopas when his head was crushed by a whiffletree. Cleopas was the second bishop of Jerusalem, and he was martyred under the rule of the emperor Domitian. Thaddeus carried the letter to Avgar of Odessa and cured Avgar of a serious illness, and Ananias the bishop of Damascus was responsible for baptizing Paul. Stephen, the protomartyr was also one of the seventy who was stoned to death by the Jews of Jerusalem. Philip, who was also known as one of the seven deacons had baptized Simon the sorcerer and Canalace's eunich and was the bishop of Asian Tralia. Others of the seven included Prochorus, the bishop of Bithynian Nicomedia and the man with the heavenly singing voice who sang religious tunes that he called hymns and who pleased everyone around him with his musical melodies; Nicanor; Stephen; Timon, another of the seven, was bishop of the island of Arabia and was martyred when he was burned by the Hellenes. Parmenas and Nicolas also made up the seven. Barnabas, who worked with Paul, was the bishop of Milan. Mark, the evangelist, was ordained bishop of Alexandria by the apostle Peter. Silas who also worked with Paul was bishop of Corinth. Luke the evangelist also travelled widely with Paul and was the bishop of Salonika, and Silvanas also preached the gospel there. Crispus, whom Paul mentions in his epistle to Timothy, was the bishop of Galilean Chalcedon. Mentioned in the epistle Romans

were Epenetus, the bishop of Carthage and Andronicus, the bishop of Pannonia, Amplias the bishop of Odissa, Urban, bishop of Macedonia, Stachys, bishop of Byzantium, and Apelles, the bishop of Heraklion. Other bishops included Phygellus, bishop of Ephesus, Hermogenes, bishop of Thracian Megara, Demas who turned against his faith, Aristobulus, bishop of Britannia, Narcissis of Athens, Herodion of Patfas, Agabus who received the gift of prophecy, Rufus of Thebes, Asyncritus of Hyrcania, Phlegon of Marathon, Hermas of Dalmatia, Patrobas of Pottole, Hermes of Philipopolis, Linus of Rome who succeeded Peter the first bishop of Rome, Gaius, another bishop of Ephesus, Philogogus of Sinope who had been appointed by Andrew the apostle, Rodion who was beheaded in Rome under Nero's reign, Lucius, bishop of Syrian Laodicea, Jason of Tarsis, Sosipater of Iconium, and succeeded there by Tertius, Erastus of Paneas, Apollos of
Caesarea, Cephas also of Iconium, Sosthenes of Colophon, Tychicus also of Colophon, Epaphras of Andriaca, Caesar of Dyrrhachium, Mark of Apollonias, Justus of Eleutheropolis, Artemus of Lystra, Clement of Sardice, Onesiphorus of Cyrene, Tychicus of Bithynian Chalcedon, Quartus of Berytus, Carpus of Thracian Berrhoe, Euodius of Antioch following Peter's rule there, Aristarchus of Syrian Apamea, Mark of Byblos, Zenas of Giospolis who was also a lawyer, Philemon of Gaza, another man by the name of Aristarchus, Pudens, Trophimus, and Onesimus. In many ways, the word of God had already reached different peoples and tribes before the apostles arrived and they merely had to reinforce the view. Converts converted others, who in turn converted new members like a multiplication table with no end. Jesus had initially appointed the seventy, some said seventy-two, in the same way that a shepherd gathers his flock of sheep, and they had teamed up and gone out to different peoples and tribes.
They had all been accorded gifts in line with their talents. Some had the gift of healing, some prophecy, and others had been accorded the gift of tongues.

Like the Baptist, they prepared the Way.

CHAPTER 13.

AD 44-48

Luke went to see Petros in Jerusalem.

He brought tidings from Ioanna, and Petros listened to the excellent work being done up north. He was about to embark on missionary work himself. James had gone off to Spain, and he had heard the Magdalene woman had gone to Gaul.
Herod Agrippa 1 was starting to crack down hard on the Christians. His reign had begun back in 37 AD, with Judea and Samaria handed to him in 41 AD following his loyalty to the new emperor Claudius, and he had already had James, one of the original four apostles arrested and beheaded. Nor had he stopped there, because in attempting to appease the orthodox Jews, he had ordered the arrest of Petros.
Whilst he was imprisoned, Petros heard from a guard that the body of James had been claimed by the Spanish family he had been having dinner with on the night of his arrest. It was their intention, or so he had heard, to bring the body with them on their return to Spain and venerate the remains.
Petros brooded on that one. He thought back to the time on the Galilee when he had recovered his grandfather's body from the water. Normally the heat of the land dictated that the dead be buried without delay, and he couldn't help wondering if Jerusalem was the proper place for his friend - perhaps on the Mount of Zion. It was something he needed to mull over.
He had a dream that night, and in it he was reassured that the proposed veneration was a good thing for the faith. He was also told to prepare for a messenger from God, an angel, who would

help him to escape. Heaven had plans for Petros that didn't include having him killed before his time. Later that night, the angel came to him, and shielded him from the sight of the guards with his cloak.
Petros was now free to continue his work. He knew it was time to leave Jerusalem.
There was a strong Christian community abiding in Antioch, and he decided to go there. He had many friends there. As luck would have it, a caravan was leaving the next morning, and he managed to find himself a place with the group. They were glad of the extra hand.
Petros found himself doing the chores of the camp; collecting firewood, taking care of the livestock, fetching pails of water from the springs and rivers.
He had always enjoyed good solid physical labour that got his hands dirty. It was one of the things he missed most about fishing.
But despite having had to leave Jerusalem, he knew the evangelization would go on. It was a heart-warming feeling.
He knew that the work of his friend James in Hispania would bear fruit for centuries to come. The Spanish family who had befriended him would honour him even onto death and were already planning to transport his remains to Santiago - the very edge of the known world. It would, in time, become known as the Camino De Santiago.
Christianity had come to Hispania.

***

It was so strange how life worked out.
Xavier had never fully recovered from the trauma of his crucifixion, and although he lived for a few years after that he had ceased his work on the seas.
He complained of pains in his bones and even in the joints of his fingers, and his feet were constantly sore. He no longer had ease of movement, and any movements he did make were wracked by

pain. He had, of course, returned to Hispania and had settled down again in Toledo with his family.

When Xia came to visit his brother he was shocked by his brother's appearance and he realised with much sadness that his older brother was not long for this world.

It was in that moment that he received the most extraordinary conversion to the faith long practiced by his brother. He asked Xavier about it and astonished his elder sibling when he announced it was his intention to get baptized. Xavier was delighted and wondered at the change of heart in his younger brother, but he knew too, and this had been reinforced by his own incredible faith, that the Holy Spirit worked in mysterious ways.

Like Xia, Xavier had an inkling that he hadn't long for this world. He sensed it deep in his bones, and he knew he wasn't breathing right. It was as though he was again on the cross, looking down at the heads of the Roman soldiers, his breathing laboured, and his limbs stretched to breaking point and bleeding from the nail wounds to his hands and feet. The agony was intense, made worse by the blinding hot sun. Thirst attacked his throat, and his tongue felt swollen and strange. The longer he hung on the cross, the worse things got. He could do nothing about insects landing on his face, except flinch, and even that became painful. Speech was all but impossible and sapped strength. His lips were dry and cracked raw under the unblinking sun. He wished for rain, but the sky devoid of cloud, was a deep bright blue. He sensed the Roman soldiers gathering their belongings and preparing to leave. He could see them through his half-closed eyes. He knew the end was near, and that the Roman soldiers would break his legs to hasten death or lance him through the ribcage before leaving. But the soldiers had been drinking and forgot.

They left, laughing among themselves at their coarse humour. He remained on the cross for what seemed an eternity, but eventually he heard voices that he recognised. Friends.

There was concern in the voices. "Is he dead?"

A gruff voice. "No, he's not. Give me a hand with this cross, will you? Grab that rope. Not that one, you clown."
He thought he was dreaming, but the voices were real and recognisable, and humour was there even in the grave circumstances.
"What will we do with him?" asked the voice which had grabbed the wrong rope.
The answer was short and rough. "We'll bring him to Luke. He'll know what to do."
Luke had helped to heal him as much as any man could, but the crucifixion had left scars both internally and externally with Xavier, and time eventually caught up with him. He had his family around him as he lay on his deathbed in Toledo. He asked for a private word with Xia.
He eyed his younger brother. "Well, brother. We've been through a lot together, sailing the high seas, spending time together as brothers should. You'll look out for my family when I'm gone?"
Xia had tears in his eyes. "You can be assured of that, brother."
"And you'll keep the faith?"
"I will."
Xavier died with a smile on his thin lips.
The conversion of Xia was very pronounced and very strong. He spent the rest of his days practicing the Christian faith as espoused by his older brother. Although married now himself with two young sons he always had time for his brother's family and was a promise he managed to fulfil.
Perhaps that was how he fell in with Luke and Paul, during the latter's missionary journeys and how he ended up on a storm-tossed boat about to be shipwrecked off the coast of Malta.

CHAPTER 14.

C.54 AD.

Luke was having a crisis of faith.

There were things he didn't understand about the life of Jesus. Why had the man always spoken about important things in parables? Parables were often difficult to understand, even for men of learning like Luke. There were times he wished Cesari were still alive, so he could discuss important matters of the day. Luke missed his father, and the talks they used to share.

Grief was hard to understand. Even knowing that there was a life beyond, didn't shield a person from grief. Jesus himself had felt grief, as had Mary. What person could shield themselves from the harsh brutalities of life? The pain was something one had to learn to live with, and sometimes that was a struggle. If not dealt with adequately, it could eat away at a person, turning them bitter and making life itself a misery - a dark morass from which there was no escape. It was an existence within an existence. It was a jail sentence with no possibility of parole. It was a cry in the wilderness that went unheeded. Perhaps unheard.

He didn't know where this crisis of faith had come from. He'd always been so sure of himself, so confident of his abilities. He'd remained unmarried in life, and he wondered now if that was the cause of his sudden malaise. Life could be a lonely business. The nature of his work had always kept him busy, particularly his mind. He'd found solace in books, in his work, in the people he had met, but like a thread going astray on a loom, he wondered now was all that enough. Was his life unravelling like a thread?

He sipped at a beer, his mood pensive. He drank very sparingly. He took a piece of flat bread and chewed slowly, his mood still pensive. Sombre almost. Why was he feeling like this?

His thoughts turned to Paul. There was a man who never had any doubts. It helped, of course, that he had been born a Roman. It opened doors that would otherwise remain closed. But Paul had been more than that. He was also a Pharisee who had been taught by the great Gamaliel, a leading and very influential member of the Sanhedrin council. In Paul's own words "he was a Hebrew born of Hebrews."

Perhaps it was the enormous undertaking in writing a gospel that was undermining his confidence. He brushed aside the food and drink and sat deep in thought. Perhaps a silent prayer was running through his mind.

He eventually moved off the stool and went outside to clear his mind. The sun was a hot orb in the pale blue sky, and the palm leaves rustled slightly in the soft breeze. He felt suddenly alive, more energetic. His feelings of negativity were dissipating beneath the hot rays of the sun.

A group of children were playing nearby. It was a game Luke remembered from his own childhood.
He chided himself for his earlier negativity.

* * *

Escobar.
Life had changed for Escobar in extraordinary ways. He was aware of a strange mysticism in his life as though Rachel was

still around, looking over his shoulders, guiding and informing his decisions. Some might have called it a sixth sense but to Escobar it was a very real, very tangible presence. It wasn't frightening, but rather comforting.

He was at a time in life when he could look back and see all that he had achieved. Perhaps it was something all men did?

He had come to love living in Ephesus with its magnificent views out over the Mediterranean. Though the land could be dry and sandy in places, there was also an abundance of greenery - palm trees in particular growing well in the sunny climate. The hot climate supplied the ideal conditions for harvesting grain and tomatoes and olives and hundreds of other foods that adorned tables in that part of the world. The women used the spices of the land to make the food, a taste unique and varied according to particular areas.

The influence of Rome was evident even in a place like Ephesus, and the Roman pillars that made up the temple at the heart of the city were a testament to man's ingenuity. Games were held in the stadium, plays re-enacted, and there was even a library of books. There were many bath houses, including outdoor ones with stone pillars in the larger pools.

He helped Ioanna with his church work as much as he could, and with the passing of time, although he never quite forgot the events of Jerusalem, he learnt to live with himself and to look forward instead of back.

He was a new man.

* * *

Xia had never found the sea as appealing after the death of Xavier, but it was a way of life he was familiar with, and he soon returned to what he knew. There was a camaraderie aboard boats that couldn't be found elsewhere, and he loved the vast vistas of the sea and pitting oneself against everything the elements could throw at you. In many ways the sea helped to heal him after his personal loss and his new faith helped him to believe that Xavier was still there, hovering somewhere over his left shoulder and watching and guiding every decision he made in life. In his heart, he felt good about returning to work and being able to support his family back in Toledo. Many of the men he worked with had also known and worked with Xavier, and they told many stories that Xia was able to laugh at.

There was something wild and alien about the sea. It was a vocation, a call to the wild. He loved the smell of the sea in his nostrils and what he regarded as the great outdoors. There was a real, tangible sense of life aboard a creaking ship, the sound of men tugging on ropes, the crackle of the wind against the sails and the way the light hit everything around - the surrounding water, the sails, the ship itself. It was enriching and no amount of silver dinarii could compensate for such a feeling of wellbeing.

In its own way the sea helped to heal Xia's mind, and the more he threw himself into his work the more he was able to get on with life. He became adept with all of the tasks aboard seagoing vessels and his expertise matched that of a master hand.

He no longer had to seek work. Ship masters sought him out, offering him top wages to work for them. It suited him, because he had two families to look after back in Toledo.

Sometimes when he travelled home, he was taken by the fact that Christianity had taken such a hold on his native town. He felt sure in his heart that Xavier would have approved. The ties of blood and brotherhood were so strong that it convinced him of this.

The tides were turning for Xia Santos.

CHAPTER 15.

48 AD.

Escobar mourned the death of Mary.

The years since the crucifixion in Jerusalem had been good ones. His new work in the schools and the church had helped to heal his mind. He had also remarried, and he had a boy and a girl from his latest marriage. At first, he had feared to remarry, fearing that he was somehow betraying Rachel. Or her memory. But he had a dream, having consulted with both Mary and Ioanna on the problem, and the dream assured him that Rachel didn't want him facing life alone.

Sarah was a different woman than Rachel. More outspoken and sure of herself. She came from the land of Arabia, her father having moved to Ephesus when she was fifteen, after securing new work contracts in the silk trade. Her style of dress was bright, and she certainly knew how to turn the heads of men. Like many women from the land of Arabia, she wore a silk veil, the niqab, over her face, only the dark eyes visible over the veil hinting at her beauty. She was a woman who knew what she wanted and wouldn't settle for less.

When she met Escobar, bizarrely at a bazaar, she instantly recognized something in him that appealed to her. She liked the level of maturity he displayed, his rugged good looks, the fact that he worked with children, and the fact that he seemed to be of good standing in his local church. She liked his friends too and believed you could tell a lot about a man by who his friends were. Their first conversation was easy at first. He was watching her as she bought spices at the market, and she was aware of his interest.

"You must like that type of food?" he suggested, with a smile.
"Sorry?"
"Hot and spicy," he commented. "Food that sings of the heavens."
Strange way of putting it, she thought, liking his smile. *Food that sings of the heavens.* She still said nothing.
He wasn't put off. "Try the cumin," he suggested. "It depends on what you're making, of course?"
"Yellowfin tuna," she said. "With anchovies, sardines and greens."
"My favourite," he lied. "Perhaps the coriander then, and pepper."
"And olives, of course."
"Of course," he agreed.
They smiled at each other, like teenagers. "And bread," he added.
"Of course," she agreed.
"My name is Escobar," he said, introducing himself. "You're new around here?"
"Sarah," she replied. "I've just moved here with my parents. From Arabia. Did you grow up here?"
He shook his head. "No. Jerusalem."
"Jerusalem? That's a long way off. How did you end up here in Ephesus?"
"That's a long story," he explained. "One best discussed over dinner."
The die was cast. He had let it be known he was available for dinner.

*　*　*

Escobar wore his finest robes for the dinner at Sarah's house. His sandals smelt of new leather and he had spent the late afternoon in the baths.
"You look nice," Sarah commented, when she saw him.
She had spent the better half of the afternoon in a comparable manner; getting her hair done and consulting with friends on proper attire and beauty oils. She looked quite stunning, and Escobar wasn't slow in telling her so.

She bade him enter.

He took the drink she offered him - the fruit of the vine - crushed grape which he drank from an earthenware cup. She only drank water, explaining she didn't like intoxicants.

The table was set, and decorated with fresh flowers and candles. The yellowfin tuna smelled delicious, and an aroma of Mediterranean spices clung to the mint scented air.

"Smells good," he said, complimenting the food.

It tasted good too, which he found out as soon as they sat down to enjoy the meal. Escobar felt very relaxed in her company, and she felt likewise as was clear by her laughter throughout the meal. She cleared the dishes as soon as they had eaten and joined him outside as he stared upwards at the starry night. Their conversation together had been light enough, with neither touching on any touchy subjects. She found out he was married before, but she decided against asking him about it. Later perhaps, when they knew one another better.

"You promised to tell me about Jerusalem," Sarah teased.

Escobar nodded, his face serious.

"You look so serious," she remarked.

"It's a serious story," he replied. He told her then of how he had grown up in Jerusalem and of how he had become involved with the Sanhedrin upon reaching adulthood. He told her something of his earlier marriage and of his feelings following the death of Rachel and his son. Mostly though, he spoke about a man from Nazareth named Jeshu whom he claimed was a son of God. He spoke of how he had a role in the death of the man, and the agony of crucifixion, and he spoke at length about the aftermath. He told her something of men like Annas and Ciaiphas and the role they had played, and the influence they had exerted over young minds. It sounded like some grand theatre played out on one of Herod's stages. She said as much, but Escobar remained serious. She could see in his eyes that he was drawing on painful memories and she wished him to stop, but like a rabbit caught in the glare of light, Escobar's story was mesmerising, and she couldn't, even if she wanted to, cut off the flow of words that streamed like blood from a wooden cross in an unstoppable deluge. She was transfixed by his words, and especially when he talked about the Resurrection. She had no doubts as to the truth of the words; there was an intent there that had to be believed.

She remained silent for a long time after he finished speaking and eventually said in a quiet voice. "That's some tale."

"We'll talk more of it tomorrow," he promised, in effect saying he wanted to see her again.

She smiled. "Tomorrow," she agreed.

CHAPTER 16.

41-54 AD

The Emperor Claudius ruled Rome from 41 to 54 AD. A childhood illness had left him with a pronounced limp, and he had survived purges of nobles started by the earlier Emperors Caligula and Tiberius.

The one man who had survived all the mayhem, and yet had a hand in a lot of it, was of course Scarpacco. Now a senator, he had over the years amassed great power, wealth and influence.

Much as a man might amass earthly treasures like land and horses, Lucius Scarpacco set out to do just that following his success in the Roman Senate in getting Cesari exiled. He breathed easier knowing that his arch enemy was gone and no longer a threat to his plans.

With the Ciccone clan banished to Greece to live out their days he soon had no more use for Marcus, but the man disappeared with his entire family before Lucius could do anything against him. Lucius made no attempts to track him down. It was in a way, a relief.

With Cesari out of the way, he cast a cold eye over Roman society to see who could further his ambitions. Life was full of allegiances and having the right connections made all the difference in life. He believed in amassing power and believed that the man with the most power was usually the one who came out on top in most situations.

He formed a friendship with Agrippina the Younger who would be known as the mother of Nero, the sister of Claudius, the adoptive great granddaughter of Tiberius, and the great granddaughter of Augustus. Despite the fact that she was seeing another man he began sending her flowers and gifts and

gradually he managed to break down her defences.
When she gave birth to Nero there was some speculation in Rome as to whether Scarpacco could be the sire because despite his attempts to keep their affair secret, such knowledge eventually got out. Rome was a city of intrigue and gossip.

Although Nero was despised as a despot, he had as Emperor installed wonderful baths for the public to enjoy. The baths were meeting places, and many a business deal was struck there. They could prove noisy at times, even raucous. Many Romans
also used the environs of the baths to indulge in sports like boxing and generally keeping fit as the physicians of the day recommended.

It was at the baths that Luke came across Marcus Aurilius, a man he thought he would never see again. The man had changed a lot since Luke had last seen him. The swagger was gone, and the man walked with a bit of a limp. He was heavier and older, but the features of his face were still recognisable. He spotted Luke almost as soon as Luke saw him, and he paused: "You look familiar?"
"You don't remember me?" Luke enquired.
Marcus shook his head. "No, should I?"
"You should Marcus. You brought me for walks when I was a child."
Marcus's eyes widened. "Luke," he exclaimed. "Luke Ciccone?"
"That's right, Marcus."
A smile came to the face of Marcus, making him look suddenly years younger. He beamed with delight.
"You betrayed my father, Marcus. You denounced him to the Senate."
The smile disappeared from the face of Marcus. "To my eternal regret, Luke. It was all Scarpacco's doing. He hated your father for something that happened when they were young soldiers together. He convinced me at the time that I was doing the right thing." Marcus paused, before continuing. "Is your father still

alive?"

"No, Marcus. He died a number of years ago."

Regret crossed the face of Aurilius. "I always liked your father," he said.

"How about your mother and sisters?"

"They live in Greece."

"Is that where you all went after your father's exile? I often wondered."

"We lived in Crete, Marcus. It was a good life. A happy place."

Marcus nodded to himself. His thoughts seemed to be miles away. "He was sorely missed in the Senate after that. Scarpacco didn't really win. He found himself shunned by certain influential men within the circle. He continued to amass power as such men do, discarding those he no longer had a use for."

"Including you, Marcus?" Luke prophesized.

"Especially me," Marcus confirmed. "I knew too much about him. I was a danger to him, and his plans. He tried to silence me in and around the time Sejanus was exposed as a traitor."

"Tiberius had Sejanus killed?"

"One of the few things he got right in the end," Marcus observed. "Sejanus had his own imperial ambitions, but he crossed the line. Scarpacco nearly fell with him."

"They were in it together?"

"Like brothers."

A silence ensued amongst the two men. Eventually Marcus eyed Luke with that old familiar grin. "You know, I'd like the chance to make up for the past. Will you join me tonight at my villa for dinner? We have much to discuss."

"Do we, Marcus?"

"Yes," he enthused. "Rome has changed a lot since you were a child. Please say you'll come. I want you to meet certain people."

"Okay, Marcus," Luke agreed. "Around seven?"

"Perfect!" Marcus beamed.

* * *

"What prompted the hate between your father and Scarpacco?"

"A massacre."

"A massacre?"

"In Judea. When they were young men. Herod the Great ordered a massacre in a little village of baby boys under the age of two."

"Baby boys?"

"He was incensed with three magi who came into his territory. Three kings. They had been guided there by a great star in the heavens that heralded the birth of a messiah. A new king."

"Herod was always a madman," commented one of the senators who'd always kept a close eye on the east.

The emperor looked at his senator. "Did you ever hear of this massacre?"

"Not the details of it. Just ugly rumours."

"I can scarcely credit it," the emperor breathed. "I want emissaries sent to
investigate. No wonder, we Romans, are hated in the provinces."

"To what end?" the senator asked. "Herod's dead."

"But Scarpacco still lives," the emperor said. "See to it man."

The senator left the room. When he had gone, the emperor picked up a decanter and gazed over the rim of the drinking vessel at Luke. "Tell me about your father?"

Luke smiled. "A true Roman. Gentle, kind, but as hard as nails when he needed to be."

"He was a senator, yes?"

"Until he was exiled."

"What happened to you then?" the emperor asked.

"We went and lived in Greece."

"After Rome, that must have been a culture shock?"

"At first," Luke admitted. "But we settled well there. It was good for my father's health too. He was stressed in Rome."

"Important duties of state, no doubt," Claudius commented shrewdly, and with some insight.

Luke nodded his head in agreement. "That and the internal politics."

"Yes," Claudius said reflectively. "It keeps us all on our toes."

"What's going to happen to Scarpacco?"

Claudius shrugged. "Perhaps nothing. He has important friends still in the Senate.

I'd need certain proof before I could make a move against him."

"He's that powerful?"

"You'd better believe it." He stood to go, limping towards the door. "Just ask Marcus here. He knows him better than most." Marcus and Luke stood as the emperor donned his cloak. Claudius looked at the two men and suddenly smiled: "But don't worry. If there's any truth to this story about Judea, he'll be finished. I'll personally see to it. Marcus, thank you for a lovely evening and a fine dinner. Most enlightening."

He limped to the door and was about to leave when a thought struck him. He glanced back at Luke. "By the way, who was the king Herod was so frightened of?"

Luke eyed the emperor. "Some say the kingdom was not of this world. The boy was Jesus of Nazareth."

"He came from Bethlehem?"

"Yes, he was born there. But his parents fled Herod's persecution and settled in Egypt. During the census, they returned to the father's place of birth - Nazareth."

"And that's where they settled?"

"Yes, emperor."

"Interesting," mused Claudius. "This Jesus of Nazareth...I have heard of him.
Wasn't he put to death by Pontius Pilate in Jerusalem?"

"Another victim of Roman rule," Luke suggested.

The emperor nodded solemnly. "You're a believer in this man?"

It wasn't a time for lying. "I am," Luke declared.

Claudius smiled. "I like a man of conviction. Without doubt, you're the son of a Roman Senator. It takes guts to admit to something like that. Especially in these enlightened times, when people who agree with your views are being thrown into the Great Arena for the lions to feast upon." His smile widened. "Goodnight, gentlemen."

* * *

Marcus smiled when he had gone. "You made a good impression

on Claudius."

"He's not the fool I was led to expect," Luke agreed.

Marcus sobered. "People would do well to remember that. It's the fault of his mother. She calls him a fool, and somehow the title struck."

"You mention his mother. Is he not married, then?"

"Not anymore. He was married to Agrippina the Younger until she was exiled by Caligula - the nephew of Claudius. She was a descendant to the emperor Augustus." The man in power before Tiberius.

"What was she like?"

"A scheming harlot. Not to be trusted. She dotes on her boy. Some say Scarpacco was involved with her."

"The son of Claudius?"

Marcus shook his head. "No. A son by a previous marriage. His name is Nero."

A shiver hit Luke as he heard that name. He didn't know why. An uneasy feeling bit into him as he heard that name, and he asked nothing further.

He'd never heard of Nero before now, and he didn't know why the name had
caused him such sudden dread. He smiled at his host. "I must be going."

"I'll get your cloak, Luke. It's been great having you here. A bit like old times."

Luke nodded. Despite his initial reservations, he had enjoyed the evening.

As he readied to go, Marcus struck out his hand. "Friends again?"

Luke looked at the hand for a long moment, and then accepted the handshake.

"Friends," he said.

CHAPTER 17.

46-48 AD.

The missionary journeys of Paul had begun. Travelling west, he began a mission of evangelicalism. Luke accompanied him.

Leaving Antioch, they sailed to Cyprus. The ship was a galley, a *boreme*, with two decks of oarsmen. The rigging of the ship had been perfected by the Phoenicians - a seagoing people and voracious traders - who hailed from Byblos, an ancient city of stone built on the Mediterranean, and a place from whence the bible got its name. History prior to 1200 BC would have referred to them as Canaanites, but in later years the Greeks referred to them as the Phoinikes. They were famous not just as seafarers and traders, but for the special purple dye they exported, and which was used in the manufacture of royal cloaks. They traded heavily from Byblos, from Tyre, and from Sidon. They exported wine, olive oil, and the famous Lebanese cider wood that was used in the construction of so many ships. They were a people who adopted so many ideas from the iconic Assyrian and Babylonian kingdoms that it led to a cultural explosion in Greece, bringing about Greece's Golden Age, and laying the foundations for western civilization to flourish.

Paul had another man with him on the trip and his name was Barnabas, and he was accompanied by a youth by the name of John Mark.

A strange collection of characters, Luke ruminated. Still, who was he to complain? They were bringing him along because of his skills as a physician.

Paul joined him on deck. "It's a bit rough," he pointed out.

Luke nodded. "Good wind for the sails though."

Paul bobbed his head in agreement and eyed him curiously.

"Don't you ever get seasick, Luke?"

A faraway look came into Luke's eyes. "Once upon a time, I did," he said reflectively. "I remember a trip to Alexander Troas with Cesari..."

"Cesari?"

"My father."

"Oh?"

Luke carried on speaking. "I remember telling him how someday I might find a cure for seasickness...hasn't happened yet." He grinned wryly.

"Maybe someday," Paul remarked, his face looking pale.

"You should go below," Luke suggested. "Always helps. Take the weight off your feet."

"Fresh air helps too."

"Sea air."

The men were silent awhile.

"Your father must have been proud of you, Luke. Qualifying as a physician?"

"Not initially. He hated the thought of it."

"How come?"

Luke's face darkened. "It was the night I was brought into the world. I was one of four. A quadruplet. They said it was complications. My mother died."

"But I thought Rebecca...?"

Luke shook his head. "She's my aunt and my stepmother."

"And they all live in Greece now?"

"Yes, except for one sister. She married a Spaniard and lives in Hispania."

"Where?"

"Toledo."

The ship lurched, and Paul grabbed Luke's arm as he staggered.

"Getting rougher," Luke commented. The sky overhead was a dull grey, and rain had begun to slant down.

"Time to retire," said Paul, weaving his way to his cabin. "Goodnight, Luke."

"Goodnight, Paul."

***

They pulled into Salimas the following day. Overnight the winds had abated somewhat, and the oarsmen had been deployed.
Rivulets of sweat drenched their torsos as the sun climbed higher in the sky. They were an able-bodied lot, fit, and with seamen's muscles. The women of Salamis were all over them as soon as they hit port. With wages in their pockets, they would drink their fair share of rum, and entertain the women.
A few of the older, wiser, married hands would stay aloof from it all. They'd still go for a rum, but often as not, would sit apart in a corner of the room at a quiet table, overseeing their younger, and more brash, brethren.
Paul was also glad to be off the ship, and back on *terra firma*. He had been quite ill during the night.
Luke had to proscribe him medications during the night.
Paul grinned at his companions. "Now the real work begins," he exclaimed, his face having regained its natural colour, and his eyes bright.
Nearby the oarsmen were also disembarking down the gangplank, their spirits high.
Paul eyed them with a narrow gaze. Luke could guess his thoughts. Trained as a Hellenistic Jew in the rabbinical schools of Jerusalem by the great Gamaliel, Paul tended to frown on their cavorting, drunkenness and their general way of life. He was grateful to them for getting them safely to Salamis, but he didn't pretend to understand their mentality. He was from a higher school.
When Cleopatra of Egypt died in 31 BC, control of Cyprus passed back to Roman hands. It had originally been part of the Roman province of Cecilia before the Egyptians took control of it. Following on from these events in 22 BC the Emperor Augustus made Cyprus one of the senatorial provinces under a proconsul of praetorian status. Roads were built by Augustus.
Paul and his party followed the southern coastal route, their final destination Paphos. Their route took them through the

THE SCRIBE

cities of Tremithous, Kitron, Amathus, Kouion, Paleapaphos, and finally Paphos itself. They preached everywhere they went to Jews and gentiles alike. In Kouion they were confronted by the pagan community at Apollo, and at Aphrodite of Paleapaphos they met with similar hostility. The pagans believed that Aphrodite was born from the foam of Uranus at this spot.

In Paphos they met direct hostility in the form of a man known as Barjesus. Paphos was the seat of the Roman government in Cyprus, but Barjesus attempted to prevent Paul and his companion Barnabbas from meeting with the proconsul Sergius Paulus who had been appointed to his role by the Roman Senate. Barjesus had been hostile in the extreme. "You want to see Sergius Paulus?" he demanded. "Why, may I ask?"

"To proclaim the good news," Paul answered.

"Good news." Barjesus grinned at his entourage, but the humour didn't reach his eyes. "What good news?"

Paul took his measure of the man. With a canny insight he understood the fear of the man. What Barjesus feared was losing his influence and prestige with the Roman proconsul.

Paul recognised the type of man Barjesus was. He preached a false gospel, and he was naturally suspicious of those whose gospel seemed to be grounded in goodness and faith. He didn't want his own work undermined. Still, Paul was determined to get his message across. He had heard that the proconsul was a wise and sagacious man who would give them a fair hearing.

Barjesus was a *'magos'*, steeped in neo-Platonism, a doctrine sharply at odds with Christianity. Babylonia had always been considered the home of magic, and it had been initially practiced by Persian priests, and then by Babylonian Jews, but the knowledge had passed down to men of dubious character who passed themselves off as sorcerers and magicians. Barjesus was such a man.

Paul realised that Barjesus was speaking again, lashing out orders to his underlings. "Seize him," he ordered, his voice harsh. "What are we to do with him?" a man asked.

"Have him tied to a pillar and scourged," Barjesus ordered. "That should shake some sense into him."

Paul didn't resist as they dragged him away. He heard Luke protesting the treatment behind him.

They tied him to a pillar, and he gritted his teeth, as a Roman soldier began the scourging. The pain was intense, but the body was wounded, not the mind or the soul. They gave him twenty lashes and left him in a bleeding heap, half-unconscious, on the ground.

Luke found him like that and undid the ropes which bound him. He bent and picked Paul up like he was a baby. Barnabas rushed to help.

Luke gave him a curt order to fetch clean linen and pails of water. They brought him into a nearby inn where the proprietor at once put rooms at their disposal. Luke laid Paul down on a bed on his stomach and worked on repairing the damaged back.

Luke checked Paul for any signs of hypovolemic shock. He then added a salt mix to the water to produce brine, which he administered to Paul's back. He cut up the strips of linen and made crude bandages which he tied around Paul. It could have been worse.

Only one *lictor* was employed in the scourging, and the whip hadn't contained any metal bits which could have cut deeper into the skin. Luke gave Paul some medicinal alcohol which helped to dim the pain. The man slept. Barjesus had known what he was doing, Luke thought sourly. The man had inflicted injuries on Paul, but he had given orders that the punishment was not to be too severe. He had known it was inevitable that Paul and Barnabas would likely get an audience with the proconsul despite his vehement objections. If Paulus saw that Paul was incapacitated because of a whipping, his ire might descend on Barjesus. The sorcerer and magician were worrying about that very point as Paul lay recuperating.

*　*　*

After Paul had lain up for a few days, Luke arranged for them to

see the proconsul. He was wise enough to bypass Barjesus. He explained to the proconsul that his father had once worked in the Roman Senate, and that knowledge at once opened doors. They were ushered into the proconsul's presence that very evening. The proconsul noticed Paul's discomfort at once.
"You don't look well," the proconsul said to Paul.
"Scourging does that to a man," Luke explained.
"Scourging? Who ordered that?"
Barjesus coughed. "I did."
"Why?" The proconsul looked perplexed.
"He preaches a false doctrine," Barjesus retorted. "He preaches a new faith...that of Christianity...it's at odds with everything we've been taught...too many new and false ideas."
The proconsul was thoughtful. "I like innovative ideas," he proclaimed. It was a rebuke to Barjesus, who flushed and sat back in his chair.
Paul restrained a tight grin. "I came to Cyprus to spread the good news about Jesus Christ. Have you heard of this man?"
The proconsul nodded. "We've heard some stories," he acknowledged. "Is it true he once walked on water and raised the dead to life."
"That's all true," Paul confirmed. "His vision..."
"Vision?" snapped Barjesus angrily. "Your visions are all false." He stood up as though to confront Paul face to face.
"And your vision is no more," Paul warned. He stretched his arm out, two of his fingers pointing like arrows towards the eyes of the sorcerer.
Instantly Barjesus was struck blind.
He flailed about unable to see, suddenly panic stricken. Paulus and the others looked at him in astonishment, and eyed Paul with a new respect.
Paulus ordered two Romans to keep Barjesus quiet. He bade Paul to a chair and said: "We will hear what you have to say, preacher." Paul talked long into the night.
The proconsul and his close circle were convinced of the truth behind Paul's words. Sergio Paulus leaned back in his chair and

clapped his hands for the servants to bring supper.

"That's some tale," he eventually succeeded in saying. "Can you baptize us in this new faith?"

"Honoured to," said Paul.

"From this moment on, Saul, call yourself Paul."

Paul bobbed his head. By allowing him to use a variation of his own name, the Roman proconsul had just paid him the highest honour he could.

Another man who had been guarding Barjesus spoke to the proconsul. "What will we do with him?" he asked.

The proconsul looked down at the blind man. He was feeling Christian.

"Fire him, and then release him out into the city."

Paul nodded at the justice of it.

* * *

Having converted souls in Paphos, Paul and his small band left on a ship the next morning and sailed for Antioch of Pisidia. They found no welcome there.

They moved on to Iconium. In Iconium they were threatened with stoning. Luke deflected that threat by suggesting they make haste for Lycaonia, and then the cities of Lystra and Derbe. So ended Paul's first missionary journey - from Derbe they returned to their starting point of Antioch. The church there awaited news of their mission.

* * *

Antioch of Syria.

Often called the 'cradle of Christianity', Antioch was an important city in Roman times. It was an important trading route between east and west. It also had a vast population. The city had been founded in the 4th century BC by Seleucus I Nicator who had once served as a general under Alexander the Great. A powerful figure, Seleucus went on to control lands subdued by Alexander as far east as India.

Antioch occupied an important geographical, military and economic centre. It encompassed part of the ancient silk trade route, the spice trade route, and the Persian Royal Road. During the Second Temple period it was also an important centre for Hellenistic Judaism. The city was recognized by Rome as a vital one.

Paul reported back to the Christian church at Antioch on the results of his first missionary journey. Luke had returned to Troas.

Eventually with the passage of time, Paul approached Barnabas and suggested a second missionary journey. Barnabas was enthusiastic, but then he suggested taking along John Mark, a young relation of his who had gone with them on the last trip to Cyprus, but who had deserted them and returned home for reasons best known to himself.

Paul shook his head. "He has no staying power...he deserted us in Pamphylia."

Barnabas disagreed strongly. Finally, Paul had enough. "If you feel that strongly about it, then take him with you to Cyprus. I'll go my own way, probably with Silas."

"May it be so, then," said Barnabas storming away.

Paul watched him go and then shook his head. He'd take Silas with him to Tarsus.

From Tarsus, they went to Derbe and Lystra, and in the latter town Paul met a man called Timothy who would accompany him for the remainder of his missionary travels. After Lystra, the three men travelled to Iconium and Phrygia. From there they travelled to Troas on the Aegean Sea, and they were joined by Luke. Paul then received a vision of a man in Macedonia pleading for help, and he at once boarded a ship bound for Neapolis. From there they went to Philippi where a woman called Lydia converts to Christianity with her entire household.

It never ceased to amaze Luke how people were converted by the preaching of Paul. In the cities of Amphipolis and Apollonia they again find an audience for their message, but they also make enemies. In Berea, people listened again, but Jews from Thessalonica arrived to stir up trouble for them. Paul travelled onto Athens, insisting this was a trip he had to make on his own, but sending for his companions later.

Athens had long been a place of great learning and influential groups lived there including the Epicureans and the Stoics and when they heard his words they brought him to the Hill of Mars so he could expound on his ideas. There was a big crowd gathered already, including the Seer.

Looking out from the Hill of Mars, Paul felt that this was the pinnacle of his missionary work. He drew himself up, controlled his breathing, and began speaking eloquently. Luke watched Paul deliver a great eulogy from the Hill of Mars and he had to marvel at the fact that Paul had been allowed to preach there. He would have agreed with Paul's assessment that this was indeed a pinnacle. This was the home of the great philosophers, and the home of Stoicism.

The Seer approached Luke. "Your friend speaks well," he stressed, indicating towards Paul with his chin.

Luke nodded smiling. "Direct from the heart," he agreed. They watched as Paul wound up his speech.

Paul was greeted to a round of applause.

After Athens he travels to Corinth and it is here that he meets a couple who will become great friends - Priscilla and Aquila.

At the end of his second missionary journey Paul again returned to Ephesus, Jerusalem, and finally Antioch.

The fathers of the church awaited his reports.

* * *

His third missionary journey started like his second, travelling again to the same places to see how Christianity was developing. After visiting the churches of Galatia and Phrygia, he decided to visit Ephesus.

Galatia was an ancient land, part of the Anatolia land mass and populated by the ancient tribes of the Tectosages, the Trocmii

and the Tolistobobii - ancient Celts who had arrived through Thrace in 278 BC. They had their own Galatian language. They had originated from the great Celtic migration led by Brennus and Leonnorios and Leotarius.
A lot of Phrygians also lived there.

Its counterpart, Phrygia, by comparison was dominated by the Phrygian peoples who were influenced by the Hittites. Their capital city was Gordium, but they also controlled Midas city.
When he arrived in Ephesus, Paul met followers of the Way, but his instincts told him there was something awry in their preaching. He drew several of them aside. "Whose name do you invoke when you speak of baptism."
"The baptism of John," one man replied.
Paul shook his head. "His baptism called for repentance from sin, but the baptism of Jesus which John himself said to follow is the one that should be practiced."
"I remember John saying something of that," another man commented.
"So do I," another remarked.
"Well, then?" Paul queried. "Are you ready to be baptized in the name of Jesus so that your preaching is guided by the Holy Spirit?"
"We're ready," they exclaimed in unison.
"Good," said Paul. "Let us go to the church of Ioanna."
The group strolled towards the church led by Paul, and as soon as they were baptized, they all received the gift of tongues. They looked at one another in amazed wonderment, filled with the Holy Spirit like men who had just enjoyed a satisfying meal together. Life was full of mystery, and they had just experienced that first-hand. They turned as one towards Paul who spread his hands and exclaimed: "Look not to me. Like yourselves, I'm simply a messenger. Go from this place and make believers of all nations."
The gift of languages or tongues was an extraordinary one, allowing the speaker a fluency that sounded like a native, and

the list of languages and dialects was as long as the Euphrates and included Hebrew, Greek, Latin, Galatian, Canaanite, Egyptian, Etruscan, Gaulish, Hittite, Old Persian, Sumerian, Arabic, and a host of other languages.

Paul nodded in satisfaction as he watched them go. His next challenge involved seven sorcerers who were under the false allusion that they could harness the same power of Paul, in relation to exorcism. When they tried to invoke the name of Jesus in one individual, they were trying an exorcism on, evil spirits turned their wrath on them and left them lucky to escape with their lives. The sorcerers were torn to pieces by the spirits, their clothing ragged and torn, their bodies bruised and bleeding, leaving each feeling as though they had just survived a session with the lions of the Colosseum. Fear engulfed them as they ran away.

Ephesus had always been a gateway to the goddess Diana, and silversmiths and merchants had made huge profits over the years manufacturing and selling Diana idols. Paul's new teaching on Christianity was beginning to usurp all that trading activity as people turned away from the worship of false idols and gods. Demetrius, one of the affected silversmiths organises a meeting of traders in which a riot breaks out and followers of Paul are seized. A city clerk, wiser than most, intervenes to prevent a bloodbath.

Sensing further antagonism, Paul decides to leave Ephesus and he travels to Macedonia. In Corinth he spent some time composing his letter to the Romans. He travels back and forth with his faithful companions, which included Luke, travelling to Troas to celebrate the Feast of Unleavened Bread.

During his last night of preaching in Troas, a young man sitting at the back of the assembly falls into a deep slumber whilst sitting on a window ledge and falls to his death. Paul follows the panicky crowd to the streets below and arrives to see one man arise and straighten and announce in anguished tones: "He's gone. He's dead."

They fall back as Paul reaches the body. Paul embraces the young man for a moment and arises and straightens himself, before announcing: "He's not dead. He simply sleeps."

The man who had pronounced death opened his mouth to issue a sharp rebuke, but the words died in his throat as the young man arose from the ground and gave them all a sheepish grin, surprised by all the commotion around him. His eyes turned towards Paul, but he had turned away, a wry smile twisting his features. To be young again, he was thinking.

He didn't know if he'd have done anything differently except maybe lose the arrogance of youth. He wrapped his cloak around him as he prepared to leave, aware of a sudden chill in the air as the sun set on the horizon.

Following further ship trips and visits to certain Greek Islands, the sun also set on Paul's third missionary journey. It was late spring, 58 AD.

CHAPTER 18.

41-54 AD

The weeping of Ramellah was about to be avenged.

Scarpacco planned a lavish feast for his birthday. His seventieth year.

It was only among the upper classes of society that birthdays were celebrated. Banquets and feasts were held to show that you had reached a certain position in life and belonged to that inner circle. The fact that the emperor had agreed to attend Scarpacco's function showed an acceptance that Scarpacco had joined the upper echelons of Roman aristocracy. Everyone wanted to be his friend.

The Emperor was still bothered by Luke's revelations concerning his host, but he was willing to concede that injustices may have been carried out for the betterment of Rome. The emperor could hardly credit the story he'd heard about Bethlehem. Nonetheless emissaries had been sent from Rome to find the truth of the matter. It would be a few months before they could report back. The meal was sumptuous. As wine was served, Torino, a young slave of fifteen broke a flute.

For a moment he froze, and then he moved to pick up the shards of glass. Scarpacco glared at the boy and issued an order to his head slave. "Seize him."

The Emperor watched astonished. The boy was grabbed by the head slave and brought to kneel before Scarpacco.

"It was an accident, Master." The boy was terrified.

"Speak only when you're spoken to, slave," Scarpacco yelped. Displeasure had suffused his face, and there was an ugly expression in the dark eyes. He made his next comments to his head slave.

"Feed him to the eels." The boy screamed in terror.

The Emperor was aghast. "It was an accident, no?" he said, addressing Scarpacco.

"So he claims," Scarpacco retorted. "But I've got to keep these people in line. Bring him to the veranda."

The pond with its flesh-eating eels rested on the veranda. Scarpacco grinned, relishing the next few moments. "Throw him to the eels. This should be good sport."

"Wait," the emperor ordered. His haughty face was shocked by Scarpacco's intentions and by the man's brutality. He turned to his secretary and quietly issued an order. The secretary dropped his wine glass and glass shattered. Orders were given for every glass in the house to be broken.

"What in Caesar's name is going on?" Scarpacco demanded.

"Would you do on to your Emperor what you have planned for this boy, now that I've committed the same crime," he said coldly.

Scarpacco stood as still as stone. His face showed shock. It was a public rebuke. The party had grown silent. The head slave released his hold on Torino and looked askance to Scarpacco. He was saying nothing. The emperor was gathering his cloaks. "Get my carriage," he ordered his secretary. "And bring the boy with you."

"Let's not be hasty," Scarpacco said. "I didn't really mean harm to the boy. It was just joshing."

"Lucicus you are a liar. If I hadn't witnessed with my own eyes what you intended doing, I would scarcely believe that a member of the Roman aristocracy could stoop so low. From this moment on you are stripped of your titles and your land. I have heard stories about your earlier behaviour whilst wearing the uniform of a Roman officer. Of these stories, I have loaned little credence to them, scarcely believing a Roman officer could act in such a way. However, today has changed my mind. I can promise you an investigation. A most thorough investigation. Emissaries have been despatched to Palestine. Should the investigation uncover your guilt, I can promise you the most severe penalty.

Do I make myself clear?"
Scarpacco was shocked. "To what do you refer?"
"Slaughter," the emperor declared. "Mass slaughter. Babies. In a small town called Bethlehem. Ring any bells?"
Scarpacco was speechless. He wanted to scream that it was King Herod's doing, but that would only betray his guilt. He would face immediate arrest. He looked around. Wild-eyed. His guests were leaving. It would be an affront to the emperor to stay when he was going. None wanted to stay anyway.
Scarpacco was finished. He was a persona non grata. The emperor had said as much. The man was like a sinking ship. Nobody wanted to be aboard when she went down. Scarpacco's face was flushed. His face sagged. How had it all gone so wrong? So quickly? As the Emperor and his guests left, his slaves retreated, fearful of his wrath. They needn't have bothered. The Napoli man was beyond caring. He threw on his cloak and stepped up on to the dais, his eyes sightless as he looked down into the pond. For a moment as he hovered in mid-air, his cloak flapping in the breeze, he looked like a trapped butterfly, wanting to fly. He hit the water with a silent splash. The eels went about their work.

* * *

Luke heard about the demise of Scarpacco from Marcus. He wondered what Cesari would have made of the news had he still been alive? No doubt the news would have pleased him, although Luke knew that his father had never been a vindictive man. He would have been pleased at the fall of the tyrant, but the death of the man, any man, was a completely different thing. "You'll be leaving shortly Luke?" Marcus asked. "For home?" Luke nodded. "Yes.my work is in Antioch. My ship leaves in two days." "We'll miss you."

* * *

More changes in Rome. Luke read the letter from his friend Marcus, and he remembered the antipathy he had felt when he first heard the name of Nero. The problem of succession had plagued the rule of Claudius, and recognising this weakness in his rule, Agrippina had conspired to have him poisoned with tainted mushrooms. The death of Claudius paved the way for her son, Nero, to assume power. According to Marcus, Nero had been overheard saying that mushrooms were the "food of the gods." It didn't auger well for Rome.

But Agrippina's actions had marked her in the eyes of Nero as a dangerous and cunning adversary who might one day conspire to have him killed. He made plans for her demise. Emperors had been wary of plots against them ever since the assassination of Julius Caesar and knew the tensions within one's family were the most dangerous. It was where treachery lurked.

CHAPTER 19.

41-54 AD

It was in the public baths that Luke's path again joined that of Marcus.

The baths had been introduced by the Romans, and they'd also had a hand in introducing giant aqueducts, stadiums and other architectural marvels that benefited mankind. The baths were the great meeting places of the day and a place where men discussed important matters of the day including politics, business matters, and sport. Many business deals had been struck in the baths, sealed with a quick handshake.

A hail greeted Luke.

It was Marcus who he hadn't seen since the dinner with the emperor. He paused, unsure about whether he should return the greeting. It was Marcus who broke the impasse, second guessing at his hesitation. "Perhaps a light meal," he suggested.

Luke thought to himself for a few moments and then he slowly agreed.

He took stock of the older man as they found a quiet corner of a local inn. Both men ordered tomato and cucumber salad, topped with feta cheese and they were given a pitcher of goat's milk with their meal.

The older man had changed little except for perhaps a tired look around the pale blue eyes and a bit of extra weight around his middle. His eyes were friendly as he looked Luke over. "You've grown a lot," he said to Luke. "Last time I saw you, you said your father was dead. Tell me about Cesari?"

"The years caught up with him, Marcus."

A film of pain crossed the older man's features. "Many years ago?"

"Ten years ago," Luke remarked, reflectively. He was surprised at the genuine remorse in the older man, and he commented about it.

The older man shook his head as though to dispel a disturbing memory. "I always liked Cesari," he explained, "but Scarpacco had such a terrible hold over me."

Luke looked at him. "Tell me about it."

Marcus hesitated, but then began talking at length about why he had felt compelled to betray Cesari in front of the Roman Senate. "Scarpacco had me in a terrible bind. My son was a gambler and one night he had a drunken brawl with a soldier from Scarpacco's cohort which led to the man's death. Scarpacco covered it up, but he let it be known that unless I worked for his interests, he'd expose the whole sorry mess. He could be very persuasive and threatening. He threatened me with ruin, my son with prison and possibly execution, and even my wife and daughters weren't immune."

"How do you mean?" Luke asked, sympathetically.

"He threatened to sell them into slavery."

Luke was silent for a time. "You should have talked to Cesari. He could have helped."

"Maybe?"

"Why didn't you try?"

Marcus shrugged. "Don't know. Pride, maybe?"

Luke couldn't help but feel sorry for their old servant. He remembered how the man had looked out for him when he was young, giving him little treats. His mind was busy as he considered ways, he might be able to help the former servant. He smiled suddenly, the answer coming to him like a divine revelation. He would use his skills as a scribe and write to Rome. He'd write to Theophilus.

* * *

Theophilus was a Roman official with a heavy background in legal affairs. He had first met Theophilus in Jerusalem when the man had been heavily involved with the Sadducees.

The Sadducees controlled the temple establishment including the all-important purse strings.

It was Luke's contention that the money they held was sometimes used to bolster their own lifestyles rather than the common good. The Sadducees persecuted the Christian movement and even Jesus had been forced to confront them. Luke also challenged them through his gospel, especially in Acts when he had discussed the parables of the good Samaritan, the unjust steward, the rich man and Lazarus, and the wicked tenants or wicked sons of Eli.

Luke's clever arguments and writings had persuaded Theophilus that his Sadducee philosophy was wrong, and Luke had also argued the point that the Levitical priesthood had effectively ended with the death of Jesus on the cross. An intelligent man himself, Theophilus recognised the logic, truth and wisdom of Luke's words. It was a sobering reflection.

Theophilus looked at Luke with a newfound respect. When he had first arrived in Jerusalem he had been persuaded by the Sadducees and their arguments that the Christian movement was somehow dangerous, but having come to know Luke, himself a learned man with a good command of languages, he now realised in the cold light of day the flaws that the Sadducees laboured under.

His friendship with Luke had grown and he had become an important benefactor to the Christian movement.

He too had changed.

**

As a chronicler of events Luke knew and understood the importance of timelines. He had taken to keeping diaries which he kept updated using the Julian calendar. The calendar had been introduced by Julius Caesar in 46 BC and was a reform of the Roman calendar.

Luke knew that an exact chronicle of events would aid his work when he set out to write Acts, an ambitious plan that was forming in his mind and a work that would rank alongside his gospel. He knew there would be an immediacy to Acts because of his faithful note keeping and the very real fact that he had seen many of the Acts himself, particularly alongside Paul in his missionary travels. His dairies often consisted of hourly breakdowns.

"In the first hour after dawn, people stirred, awoke and washed, preparing for the day ahead.

In the second hour, the women of the household would go to the wells to draw water and prepare for cooking. They would balance huge urns of water on their heads as they moved beneath the blasting rays of the summer sun.

In the third hour, there would be a call to prayer as men gathered to pay homage to God."

And so on!

Thinking of Paul he wondered what was to become of the missionary giant. He was intelligent enough to recognize the fact that Paul was making enemies, and he realised that things could turn badly against them if brought up on charges.

The knowledge strengthened, rather than weakened him and he gave a wry grin as he picked up his quill. He thought of all the wonderful people he had met on the path of Christianity, and he felt truly blessed.

He turned back to his work.

CHAPTER 20.

54-68 AD

The ancient city of Caesarea Maritima lay straddled, overlooking the Mediterranean, on the coastal way between Tyre and Egypt. An administrative capital of Judea since 6 AD, the city had been built by Herod the Great, and was a major headquarters for Roman soldiers stationed throughout Judea, Syria, and other places. It was also a place where many trials took place and was in the Roman province of Samaria.

Agrippa was the last prince of the house of the Herod. He ruled over his kingdom with Berenice, his sister with whom he lived in an incestuous relationship. She had inherited some of the looks of her great grandmother Salome, the dancer who had caused the death of the Baptist. She was just as cunning and her hold over Agrippa was immensely powerful.

Agrippa 11 was a king disliked by his subjects. The Jews hated him because he disposed of the High Priests on a whim; he was partially responsible for the outbreak of the First Jewish Roman war of 66-73, helping to support Vespasian with troops, archers and cavalry. He also supported Titus, the son of Vespasian.

Luke listened to the diatribe from the crowd as the trial time approached, trying to gauge their mood.

"What's his crime?" one man asked. "Christianity?"

"He'll get no justice from Agrippa," said another.

"Agrippa?" another man laughed contemptuous. "He's just a puppet...it's Berenice he has to watch out for. She's a viper."

"Festus has already ruled on Paul," said another. "Agrippa won't change anything, and neither will Berenice."

The auditorium at Caesarea was filling up. Agrippa and his sister were dressed in the finest of robes, purples and reds. Many of their entourage were similarly attired. Agrippa raised his hand, signalling for silence. His voice when he spoke had a stentorian air. "What say you to these charges levelled against you, Paul?"

Paul's voice carried on the evening wind. "I am a Pharisee," he exclaimed. "When I was younger, I used to persecute the Christians."

"What manner of change came over you?" Agrippa asked.

"I encountered the Risen Jesus when I was on my way to Damascus."

"You say Risen? Risen from what?"

"Risen from death," Paul answered in a loud clear voice. His answer caused a commotion in the crowd listening.

When silence had descended again upon the crowd, Agrippa asked another question. "How can this be? No man can raise himself from the dead."

"This man could. He was the Son of God."

Again a commotion broke out amongst the crowd.

"Perhaps he was merely sleeping?" Agrippa suggested. "You all thought him dead, but he was merely unconscious?"

Paul shook his head. "He died," he said emphatically. "He suffered death by crucifixion at the hands of Pontius Pilate and the Romans, was buried, and on the third day he arose again, just as the prophecies had said he would. The same people that condemned Him are the ones who are now trying to condemn me. Therefore, I appealed to Caesar. My Roman citizenship allows me to do so."

Agrippa raised his eyebrows and turned to Berenice who simply shrugged. Pontius Pilate was a name they were familiar with, but Agrippa was puzzled. "This was nearly thirty years ago?" he queried.

"Yes." Paul didn't elaborate further.

Agrippa shook his head. "I see no crime here," he announced. "However, I can't let you go. You've appealed to Caesar, and to Caesar you shall go. In the meantime, you will remain under house arrest until passage can be arranged to Rome. Have you any special requests?"

Paul considered this last question. "If I'm to go to Rome, I'd like to be accompanied by a few friends. One is my personal physician - Luke.
Agrippa pondered for a moment, and then stood to go.
"Request granted," he decreed.

*　*　*

Nero.
A schemer and a plotter and a despicable ruler. Ruling from 54 to 68 AD, he was destined to be the last ruler of the Julio-Claudian line. He had been adopted by his grand uncle Claudius and was heir to the throne as soon as Claudius had died. His imperial name was Nero Claudius Caesar Augustus Germanicus and his first few years in power were mundane enough as he concentrated on trade matters, diplomacy, and cultural matters. Historians and scribes were following his every move the historian Tacitus who already had a dim view of Nero. Some of his people regarded Nero in a good light, but others saw in him the makings of a despot. There had been some military successes under his reign; his general Corbulo had conducted a successful war and negotiated favourable peace terms with the Parthian Empire and his general Suetonius Paulinus had crushed a revolt in Britannia. Rome loved military success.
It was a city built on the Tiber. Legend had it that twin brothers, Romulus and Remus, sons of the god Mars and descendants of the Trojan hero Aeneas had been suckled by a she-wolf after being abandoned and had then decided to build a city. The brothers had argued and much as Cain had slew Abel, Romulus had killed Remus and the city had been named after him - Rome! It was a city built on blood, and throughout its turbulent history its emperors had tended to align themselves with Mars - the Roman god of war. Nero was no exception to this, fully aware of the power he yielded and unafraid to use it.
Nero was suspicious of anything that had the potential to usurp his power or anything that would upset the gods, and so

he viewed the rise of Christianity in the east with mounting concern and he sent out emissaries and spies to report on this new sect.

They reported back to Nero that the movement seemed to report back to one man - Petros of Antioch. They had also heard he planned to visit Rome soon.

Nero smiled savagely.

He looked like a dog about to bite deep into a bone. There would be no hiding places in Rome for Christians. He would see to that. Rome was his.

CHAPTER 21.

60 AD.

Storms at sea are always frightening experiences. The waves seem to take on a life of their own, and the ship rises and falls with the mood of the sea.

Paul had warned the master of the vessel, but his pleas had fallen on deaf ears. The master was a stubborn individual, confident in his own abilities to survive anything that the Mediterranean or Adriatic could throw at him. A seasoned sailor he'd never been thrown by a patch of rough weather at sea yet.

The ship itself was an Alexandrian grain vessel with nearly three hundred souls aboard. Paul had been allowed to bring some helpers including Luke, his physician. He had certain privileges even though he was a prisoner, because of his Roman citizenship.

The rough conditions began almost as soon as they set sail. The wind howled and shrieked like a banshee released from a lunatic asylum, and the boat rolled and pitched, and was tossed about like it had been flung from the angry hand of God. Water lashed the boat from all sides, even as high as the bridge, and the decks were awash. Because of the obvious dangers the master ordered everyone but essential crew below decks, lest they be lost overboard. He wasn't taking any chances there, at least.

Virtually everyone on board, except maybe for the master and some of his more hardened crew, were feeling the effects of the rough weather. Paul didn't have a good feeling about the fate of the ship, but beyond protesting there wasn't much he could do about the situation.

The rising seas threw them about like ragdolls. Luke had to attend one sailor who broke his arm when he fell against a bulwark.

One man working aboard was Xia Santos and like Paul he had reservations about the weather. His pleas to the master also fell on deaf ears. Years of experience had taught Xia what to watch out for with high seas, navigation matters, and he was something of an expert at reading clouds. He knew a cumulonimbus or thunderstorm cloud when he saw it and he saw them now.

Xia was like a lion in the arena when the storm broke the back of the ship. The waves had gotten progressively worse as the night wore on, and even the master of the ship had a worried scowl on his features. Xia managed to save numerous lives and, in the end, although the ship foundered and was lost, no lives were lost. Xia worked like a maniac, using his seamanship skills and knowledge of rope knots, employing the reef knot to help save lives. It was in a time of crisis that he showed what he was capable of. His knowledge of ropes and knots was staggering - reef knots, figure of eight loops, the two half-hitches, the anchor bend and the double bowline knot - being just some of the knots he commonly tied.

It helped that he was built like a powerhouse with massive, big shoulders and a barrel like chest packed with hard muscle. There's no doubt that if he had been crucified instead of Xavier, his iron constitution would have enabled him to survive better. Of that, there was no question.

The ship had foundered in shallow waters, which enabled swimmers to struggle ashore. Luke moved amongst them as they lay spent on the beach, administering medical aid. The master of the vessel remained in a kneeling position on the sandy shore, unable to take his eyes off his stricken ship. He looked as broken as the vessel which the merciless sea was still pounding and breaking up. There was the sound of wood splintering even above the deep howling of the wind, and its piercing, keening sound.

As the dawn approached and the sun made its tentative rise in the east, a Maltese fisherman and his young son came across the

stricken survivors and immediately summoned aid.
They had been lost, but now they had been found again.

* * *

Malta was a beautiful little island.
Its food was influenced by its location, and there were heavy Sicilian influences in the many fish dishes. The deep waters of the Mediterranean supplied an extraordinarily rich bounty and the hot sun on the land was ideal for growing olives, vegetables and fruits. The proximity of Tunisia and the wider sub-continent of Africa also influenced the way of life in Malta.
The inhabitants were small in stature but a hardy lot who went out of their way to help the shipwrecked sailors. They set up a temporary camp on the beach bringing along tents, blankets, food and water. More than one man found himself taken into a Maltese home, where the doors were open and welcoming.
Never one to miss an opportunity, Paul used the circumstances to evangelize as many of the natives as he could. They listened to his tales eagerly, hungry for news of the outside world. The land had been settled by the Sicani in 5200 BCE, stone age farmers and hunters from Sicily in Italy. Due to its superb location for shipping, it had been conquered and ruled by many factions including the Phoenicians, Carthaginians, and the Romans.

* * *

Rome.
It was a city where Christianity was already flourishing, and a man called Linus was already overruling the church that had been set up there. Linus had been ordained by Paul, but he also knew Petros and was a friend to both. So, in a sense Paul wasn't bringing Christianity to Rome; it was already there. He was just cementing the beliefs that had been started by other Christians. Coupled with the teachings of men like Linus, Paul was merely reinforcing the faith, knowing all too well the fickle nature of

man.

Paul's journey to Rome came to be known as his fourth missionary journey.

It was a journey made under captivity, and chained to the galleys to make better speed. But there were also times when they had a good wind on the sails, and they were left unshackled and free to roam the vessel.

* * *

Once again Paul found himself in chains as their new vessel docked in Ostia Antica, the harbour of Rome. A smell of fish clung to the still, fetid air. The dock was a hive of maritime activity, with vessels loading and unloading. Nobody paid much heed to the prisoners in chains, such sights being commonplace following successful Roman forays. If they had concluded anything, they'd probably be surmising that the majority were bound for the Colosseum, and they showed indifference and little pity. To many the Colosseum was a form of sport and entertainment and a good family day out.

Paul's first trial in front of Nero was about to begin. Two men on the dock did take heed of the prisoners. Petros and Linus watched in grim silence as Paul was led away. Luke noticed the two men, but his face remained impassive. It paid not to be too impulsive. Friends needed to be protected from the prying eyes of the Romans.

As a Roman citizen, Paul could enjoy certain privileges and he was given a villa to stay in with just a light guard. His friends, including Luke, were allowed to stay nearby.

Nero had never met Paul before and so had no reason to fear him. He ordered the guard to bring Paul before him before the commencement of the next games.

The appeal to Caesar was about to begin.

CHAPTER 22.

60-68 AD

The appeal to Caesar.

Paul was brought in to face Nero in chains.

Nero was there on his throne surrounded by his entourage, eating grapes and other types of exotic fruit. He was wearing a toga and sandals, and the women around him were dressed in the stola.

As the chained figure of Paul approached, Nero grinned at his entourage and opened the questioning. "They tell me you're a Roman citizen? Why then, do you persist in preaching against Rome?"

"Rome? What is Rome compared to the Kingdom of heaven?"

"You tell me."

"Rome is a city made by men and ruled by men. Heaven has been forged by the hands of God."

"Which God? Mars? Jupiter?"

"The God of all mankind. The heavenly father of Jesus."

"Ah, yes. This Jesus you preach of...wasn't he a man...a Nazarene?"

"He was much more."

"In what way? Didn't he die in the same way as other mere men?"

"He did."

"Well then?"

"He rose from the dead. After three days, he was resurrected."

"Nonsense," said Nero. "Absolute nonsense."

"Truth," Paul persisted.

"You honestly believe this?" The astonishment on Nero's face was absolute.

"Yes." Adamant tones.

Nero went into a huddle with his entourage. They conversed in hushed tones, but it was plain to see that they couldn't agree.

Paul overheard some of the conversation. "Case against him is weak...have him followed...he's a Roman citizen and can't be crucified."

Eventually the argument ceased, and all eyes turned to Paul as Nero began to speak. "You have appealed to Caesar, and Caesar has now decided. The case against you is weak, but not entirely without foundation. We have decided to release you on license, but if you come before us again, we will not be so lenient, and you will face the harshest penalties of the law. Go, in Nero's name and sin against us no more."

* * *

Paul's fourth missionary journey took in Hispania.

He had been released on license by Nero with strict orders not to practice his faith. But Paul listened only to a higher power, a power beyond this world. He could no more have obeyed Nero than he could denounce his own faith.

He was committed to the path he had set out upon. Men, like Luke, who had an equal belief, helped to reinforce his own stubborn belief. The years of missionary travel were beginning to tell on Paul, and he knew deep inside himself that he was closer to the end than the beginning. Like all mortals he would have liked to have lived longer, a lot longer, to see how everything panned out. But he knew his days were numbered.

What he feared even more than death were schisms and how the word could become distorted over time.

In many ways he was reinforcing what James had already accomplished in Hispania.

Paul strongly suspected Nero was having him followed, because he had spotted strangers surreptitiously taking notes of what he had to say. His sixth sense was warning him that his life was in danger. He had the feeling that his enemies were closing in around him. His instincts told him it must have been the same with men like the Baptist, Stephen the Protomartyr, James and Jesus who had all known their fate beforehand, but the knowledge of that didn't make it any easier to face the unknown that all mankind feared - death.

To mere mortals it all seemed so final, and consequently so terrifying. Hadn't Jesus himself appealed to his Father to let the cup bypass him? On reflection though he had also conceded: "Let thy will be done."

Paul's thoughts turned to Stephen whose stoning he had seen, and he reflected ruefully that there was a man who had known how to face death. He remembered how the protomartyr's face had lit up as he exclaimed to the crowds: "Behold the Lamb seated at the right hand of God."

The words had sealed his fate. The crowd had turned nasty, easy to ire if they suspected blasphemy, and easier still to turn to violence. They had stoned Stephen until he fell dead at their feet. But still, on what was considered his fourth missionary journey he helped to seal the word in Hispania. He stayed for some time in Hispania, a place that amused him whenever he spotted the inhabitants engaging with bulls. He couldn't understand bullfighting and why they risked life and limb to avoid the piercing horns of the irate beast.

He liked Hispania with its numerous palm trees and a landscape that in parts reminded him of Jerusalem. He found the people simple and pious, and ready to hear his word.

It was like a great hunger hanging over the land - a thirst for knowledge. They listened to his message, and they believed. They began forming their own Christian movements and praying to Paul's God. They found that their prayers were answered, in abundance. They found strength in the new concept of mass and the ceremonies that accompanied it - baptism, communion, confirmation, marriage, and finally death.

They seemed to grasp immediately the concept of the breaking of the bread and drinking of the fruit of the vine, perhaps because those staples were a vital part of their own diet. They

were encouraged by the message of a life beyond, a paradise.
They were impressed not just with Paul, but by his companions including Luke, and they remembered the teachings of James. The words resonated with them even more than the miracles which sometimes went with the words. It was a message that they found easy to believe and one which they took to heart.
They liked the fact that they could combine their new faith with their many fiestas. Veneration of the mother of Jesus was particularly strong and the people identified with her suffering in a unique way.

***

Linus had been encouraged in his faith by Petros who had arrived in Rome from the church at Antioch a few years before Paul finally arrived. Although they were destined to die a martyr's death together, Petros and Paul hadn't always seen eye to eye. Linus knew they had had words back in Antioch, but he was intelligent enough to recognize that both were on a similar trajectory but the way they delivered their message was at odds because they saw things differently. Perhaps it was due to their very different upbringings. Paul had been taught in a rabbinical school and he had a vision of things that was quite different to that of Petros whom he probably recognised as an illegitimate fisherman from Galilee - a backwater when compared with cosmopolitan Jerusalem. Cities always prided themselves above rural areas especially in learning and cultural matters. Linus realised that cities were really a reflection of what happened in the core of a country. It was the feeling of people that was different and perhaps a harking back to the old feudal and tribal rivalries that created warring feuds amongst like-minded individuals.
Linus had been born in Tuscany in Italy. Upon reaching adulthood he had travelled widely, and it was through his travels that he had come across Christianity.
He had talked to the church elders about the direction of the

church should anything happen to Petros and Paul. He had been groomed to take over the running of the church by Petros, and he had been trained with Clement who was another man ready to step up to the plate if called upon to do so. The church was making contingency plans, and Linus was ready in body and soul. He worried about Paul and Petros.
He had heard ugly rumours that Nero might not allow them to live.

CHAPTER 23.

66AD.

They had come for Paul in the same way that Jesus had been taken, at night when his defences were down. This time there were no niceties. They chained him and bundled him aboard a boat bound for the foot of Italy and they carted him off along the Appian Way towards Rome.

He was no longer allowed to preach, and his guards were rough with him. Upon reaching Rome in the dead of night he was brought to Mamertine prison, a cold, dank place of incarceration and a million miles from the villa he had received during his last imprisonment.

It meant only one thing. He was to be condemned. He could see his fate in their eyes. They had amassed the evidence against him, and they were more confident of convicting him. They knew he was no friend of Rome. He had defied the emperor. There would be no further mercy. He wasn't alone in his captivity. Christians thronged the dungeon he was thrown into, and in the corner, he saw a man leading a group of them in prayer.

It was Petros.

Paul smiled. He hadn't always seen eye to eye with Petros but acknowledged that Petros was the friend of Jesus and the leader of the church.

It was comforting to know he was in such good company. Petros smiled at him as he crossed the stone floor and knelt at his mass. His head bowed. He was ready to accept his fate. There was no fear.

* * *

A black pall of thick acrid smoke hung over Rome.
It was so thick; it sucked every bit of oxygen out of the air.
66 AD. Fire! The Great Fire of Rome. Nobody knew for sure where it had started, but the flames fanned out in all directions engulfing man and buildings alike. The fire sucked the oxygen out of the air, making it difficult to breathe. Heavy smoke coiled over the city, blackening everything. Even the sky was obscured. A heavy odour clung to the city. The smell of death. The fire was no respecter of persons. It took noble and poor alike. Animals, like horses were trapped in stables, and whimpered and threw up their feet in panic, but perished, nonetheless. Houses and buildings caught light and burned with unabashed shame. Orange flame licked the darkest corners of the city amid the crumbling ruins. Nero was furious. He saw it as a chance to blame the Christians. Orders were issued. "Arrest all the Christians. Arrest their leaders."
Petros and Paul were led in. Both were chained. Nero sneered at them. "You two are the leaders of this rabble." He waved his hands at the assembled prisoners, who stood huddled, few meeting the eyes of the emperor. They knew their fate. Paul stood up for them.
"Spare them," he pleaded.
Nero was shaking his bullish head. "Ah no," he exclaimed. "They'll go to the lions."
"And us?" Petros asked.
Nero smiled. It wasn't a pleasant smile. "You two will be crucified." A look of anguish crossed Petros's face. "I don't deserve to go like my Master." "Your Master?"
"Jesus Christ, my one true Master!" "And mine," Paul asserted.
Nero's face changed. "I am your Master," he bellowed. His nostrils flared in anger, and his eyes bore into the two men in front of him, daring them to retort. They said nothing. To Nero's chagrin. He was speaking again. "This great city has been destroyed by the fire, houses levelled, great buildings, homes and lives lost. You will all pay with your lives." Petros and Paul still said nothing. Nero looked at them thoughtfully and issued

special orders to his men. "Take them," he ordered. "And crucify them. On the highest hill. Let the city see them. And as they've turned this city upside down, crucify them that way as well."
"Emperor?" The executioner looked aghast, like he had received an impossible order.
"See to it, man," Nero ordered, calling to his head-slave to bring a bowl of cold water. Nero washed his hands as the two men were led away. In the forum below, the other prisoners were carted away to await their fate.

***

Jesus had warned him years before. "One day men will lead you where you do not wish to walk."
Roman executioners now marched them to the highest hill. The hill was steep, and the crossbeams heavy, but Petros knew they had it easier than that of Jesus. They hadn't been flogged like Jesus, the whip marks so deep and penetrative that his bone had protruded. Nor had they been forced to endure the wicked pain of a crown of thorns. Their steps were heavy because man liked to cling to life, but their hearts were light. In a strange way, it was gratifying and comforting, to die with a friend. He could sense Paul's steadfastness. His breathing was somewhat laboured. At the top of the hill, they were allowed a moment.
"And though I shall walk through the valley of the shadow of death." Paul said.
"I shall fear no evil," Petros finished for him, a brief smile flickering across his features. Both men shook hands. "Peace, brother," Paul said. "Beyond." "And to you, Paul."
Petros nodded solemnly as the executioners separated them and drove the nails home into the hands of Petros. Paul was to undergo a different fate. A man stood nearby with a sword in his hand. In the end objections had been made about crucifying a Roman citizen.

***

The agony was intense. Petros's mind had gone elsewhere. Back to Galilee, back to his family. Before his eyes closed for good, he was granted a vision. Way into the future. Crowds gathered, somewhat like today. But horror didn't mask their faces. They looked happy. Attired strangely, but happy. The cenotaph looked upright, in place. A man appeared above the crowds. Petros could see stone statues, akin to the Roman Gods of old. But the statues were of men he knew. Paul, John, and all the apostles. The man was giving a blessing. An Easter blessing. The vision showed him a successor. A Polish Pope. A popular Pope. A man of God. He hung there for a moment, with a bird's eye view, the keys of the Kingdom dangling in his hands. The promise of Jesus fulfilled. Petros smiled and closed his eyes.

* * *

Nero's revenge didn't just die with Petros and Paul. Christians were rounded up in giant sweeps and purges, given mock trials and put to death. Many died in the Colosseum, torn to shreds by hungry lions, whilst others were tied to stakes surrounding Nero's palatial home and set alight as though they were candles set up to illuminate Nero's party nights whilst he played mad tunes on his fiddle.

Many Christian movements were forced underground and symbols like the fish were used to advertise their faith.

But the days of Nero were numbered and his persecution of Christians was coming to an end. New Emperors were waiting in the wings. Four to be exact - Galba, Otho, Vitellius, and Vespasian - all destined to become Emperor in what would become known as the year of the four Emperors. Vespasian's son Titus then followed in his stead, setting up the Flavian dynasty in doing so. Domitian would then follow him.

Nero died by his own hand and his death sparked a bloody civil war in Rome. Galba, and then Otho were brought in as emperors, but they didn't last long. A new dynasty began with Vespasian because he had a direct heir in Titus. It would usher in a period of stability.

CHAPTER 24.

C. 75 AD

The children of Escobar and Sarah had been brought up as Christians. Daniel the Elder and Aniko practiced their faith diligently. Daniel was older than his sister Aniko by four years and he looked out for her when their parents died. Escobar had died first, succumbing to heart failure, and Sarah had died shortly thereafter from a broken heart.

Aniko favoured her mother, Sarah. She had the same olive-skinned look of her mother and other Saudi Arabian women, though her features were mostly hidden behind her veiled hijab. Although steeped in the new way of Christianity, Aniko still adopted the old practices. It made life somewhat easier and didn't attract hostility.

Steeped and mired in the ways of his father, Daniel the Elder became a rabbi to his people, and he continued the work of the schools that had been started by his parents following their trip to the kingdoms of Judea and Samaria and the Northern Kingdom. He favoured his father in looks, with the same sombre dark looks and lank black hair and brown eyes that hinted at a Judean bloodline. He was more squat than his father had been, probably because he had a greater penchant for studying rather than the outdoors, but he was recognised by his peers as having a solid understanding of both the Torah and the Christian way of life. He worked tirelessly for the poor, collecting old sandals so that they could walk with some measure of pride.

Aniko helped her brother in this regard although she had a more carefree attitude to life and didn't take things as serious. She married at an early age and took things a bit more seriously when she started having children of her own. What really

changed her outlook though was a battle with an illness that nearly claimed her life.
Daniel had prayed for her, even pleading with Escobar and Sarah to use their influence if they had any.
It must have been so.
As he watched his sister recover, Daniel took time out alone. He walked up into the hills and came across a tiny little cottage where the mother of Jesus had lived. He remembered being brought there as a child.
It had the sense of the sacred. He knelt in the dirt and looked skyward. He prayed silently. Then he bowed his head and his lips moved. He said only one word and that was enough. The wind whistled through the treetops.
The word was Amen!

* * *

Escobar found himself in a heavenly paradise.
He liked this new world. It was full of light, and there were different spheres and orbits. Music was everywhere, even the blades of grass seemed to move in a musical harmony. The music reached deep into the soul, stirring it. He wanted to shout for joy.
There were many levels to this new world.
Angels were present, and they had their own hierarchical order. The ones closest to the Supreme Being of God were Seraphim, known as angels of love. Next in line were Thrones who imparted understanding and Cherubim who imparted wisdom.
Powers were angels of harmony and peace, and Dominions gave out mercy and forgiveness. Both group of angels fed into Virtues which mirrored beauty. Archangels were full of glory and splendour, and Angel Princes or Principalities represented victory. The foot soldiers were simply angels who represented the first steppingstone to heaven, just above the barrier of time and space and the physical kingdom of mankind, animals, plants and minerals.
His son by his first marriage was here in this new world - Daniel

the Younger. He lived in a special palace in heaven, reserved exclusively for children because he had died as a child. Escobar had visited the palace and marvelled at how it was imbued with the most incredible light and colours.

The immediacy of this new world astounded him. There were many whom he had known in life, and many more he hadn't but who somehow seemed to know him. He was surprised by the fact that so many sages and wise counsel sought him out to seek his viewpoint on the crucifixion. He was left with the impression he was unique; men like Ciaiphas or Annas couldn't be consulted because they were not part of this new world. That was the impression that was conveyed anyway.

The senses were all enhanced in this new world. There was a scent to the flowers and trees that smelled like a very exotic perfume. Everything was sublime and food and drink tasted delicious. Water flowed in abundance and teemed with fish. The sense of sight showed that everything glowed and the sound of everything was in total harmony with its surrounds. Escobar marvelled at how touch was so different too. If he touched a blade of grass, it was as though he became at one with the blade, as light as a feather blowing softly in the wind.

The presence of Jesus was everywhere too. If you wanted space, he gave it; and if you wanted his presence, he was there for that too.

Time didn't matter in this place. The ability to move with ease just by thinking about it was staggering. It was as though one could fly. One could move back and forwards through time and space, learning about other worlds.

Schools and centres of learning were everywhere and people who had had a common thread in life on earth often gathered together like one huge gossip club or book circle; brought together to listen to one of their brethren who had conquered their particular field or who could offer new insights. There were vast libraries where innovative research could be carried out. There were wisdom parlours where one could increase one's understanding of a people or nation.

And everywhere light.

There were worlds like earth and that spoke different languages. Everyone entering those worlds had the gift of tongues or the ability to converse or simply pass messages in a clairvoyant sort of way. Like earth, there were also earth like features - mountains, streams and rivers, wooded areas, meadows and brooks.

It was amazing how much life was similar to that previously lived, with the same types of work, similar pastimes and hobbies, the same family and friendships, and enhanced levels of education. Music was everywhere, as were the creative arts - painting, poetry and writing. Writing was normally done on golden scrolls, which were categorized and stored in the giant libraries by flocks of angels. They always seemed to be the busiest in paradise, always rushing around, with a million things to do. Despite all that they seemed joyous in their toils and often sang as they toiled. It was a happy place.

In paradise, Escobar found he still had both wives, a bit like the Bedouin on earth who were allowed four wives anyway. He didn't find it too strange that both had become friends even though they hadn't known one another on earth. The love he'd had for both had travelled with him to this new place. The bonds of marriage were just as strong, if not stronger. Their love for him remained as steadfast as ever. Love and friendships were everywhere in this place; hatred simply didn't exist.

He was shown the power of prayer and how it really could move mountains. They were like millions of colourful butterflies flying over a scented meadow, their wings beating a silent entreaty directly to God. He was shown the power of tears, and how each droplet was stored in sacred bottles and dispensed to cure ills. He was shown magnificent scrolls outlining the lives of the righteous, including the many saints.

Feast days were always celebrated in paradise. People would attend in their finest robes and togas. Special talks or lectures would form a part of the ceremony and could be delivered by several channels - through song and music, or muse and poetry, or through people enacting the events on stage - ancient theatre. Humour was very evident. Even elements of black comedy and satire.

A couple sought him out one day when he was in the Halls of Wisdom. The woman spoke first. "I'm Sarah," she said, introducing herself. "This is my husband Ibrahim."

"Same name as my wife," Escobar thought. He wondered at the nature of their business with him.

"We lived in Egypt," Sarah explained. "In the shadow of the Sinai."

"Where Moses received the Ten Commandments?" Escobar's interest was piqued. He had seen Moses one day in paradise on a giant white horse, lightly holding the reins in one hand, a giant staff in the other. A large number of warrior angels had followed in his stead, each astride magnificent horses.

"That's right," Ibrahim confirmed. "We met Jesus there. He stayed with us, helped me fix a door, and ate with us."

"Interesting."

"When we eventually went to his homeland Galilee, people said he'd been put to death in Jerusalem."

Escobar's face clouded. "Yes," he said dully. "I had a hand in that." Sarah reached out a hand and touched his arm. "We're not here to condemn or to dredge up painful memories for you. What we look for is enlightenment and you can help us there. Will you tell us about Jerusalem?"

Escobar began telling them about that time, a memory surfacing of the night on earth when he had told his Sarah the exact same story. He didn't embellish anything, nor did he deny his own role in the proceedings. As he began speaking, he noticed other spirits moving in to hear him speak, interested in what he had to say. Jesus even appeared briefly, smiling at Sarah and Ibrahim, and giving a smile of encouragement to Escobar. "Speak well, my son. My people wish to learn more about the Passion."

Escobar nodded and spoke at length, and he noticed there were even saints in the audience. Somebody asked a question and Escobar suddenly realised that it wasn't directed at himself. He whirled.

Mary, the mother of Jesus, was there. He hadn't seen her arrive. She smiled at him and told the crowd about Escobar's arrival in Ephesus and of how he had helped Ioanna with the church there. The crowd looked forward to the day when they could speak directly to Ioanna about these matters, but he hadn't yet completed his spiritual mission and wasn't of this realm yet. When they asked Mary when this would be, she smiled enigmatically, but she didn't give a direct reply. "Who knows the way of the Father," she sang. It was a chorus they knew well, and they knew better than to ask further. They began to break up.

Escobar was astonished. There seemed to be millions of them. He asked Mary about it. "Many are interested in learning more about my Son. They weren't alive in that time, so naturally they wish to learn more. Even our Heavenly Father listens," she explained, and she waved her hand as though parting a huge stage curtain. Instantly, Escobar could see a giant ear cocked in their direction. Sensing a possible tremble in Escobar, Mary reached out a comforting hand. "Be not afraid, my son. Our Heavenly Father is pleased with your words and says you teach well."

She faded into the background as Sarah and Ibrahim approached him again with smiles of understanding on their faces. Ibrahim told him a story of how Jesus had used his carpentry skills to help him with a door.

Escobar listened politely, remembering all the examples he'd seen in this new world of exquisite tables and chairs and staircases. The wood was hewn and ancient and durable. Everywhere he went there were gangs of men working on different structures, constantly expanding the paradise. When he heard the full details of how the visit had altered the lives of Ibrahim and Sarah and the orphanages, they had set up following their return to Egypt, he whistled and remarked: "It was more than a simple door he worked on that day. It was a door of redemption, a doorway to another world."

The couple nodded at his assessment, agreeing fully.

Escobar came across another lecture another day, again in the Halls of Wisdom. The Halls weren't all indoors, but had huge arenas bathed in light and looked a bit like the *'stadion'* that the Romans had been so adept at building. The man was speaking about his homeland of Hispania, and he explained that he had been called Xavier. He told them wonderful tales of his land, but he also had tales of the sea and distant lands. He spoke at length about his brother, a man called Xia. The crowd looked forward to meeting him. Xavier really caught the attention of the crowds when he explained that like Jesus he too had been crucified by Roman soldiers. He spoke eloquently about the suffocating agony of the cross and of how he was lucky to survive such an ordeal.

"You must have had a good doctor?" one man suggested.

Xavier nodded. "A man called Luke. One of the gospel writers."

The crowd stirred, wanting to speak to Luke, but he was not of this Kingdom yet. Xavier was still speaking, holding up his hands so they could see the wounds of the nails, and a wry smile twisting at his lips as he commented with dry humour: "Of course, it all took its toll. That's how I ended up here talking to you good folks."

The crowd laughed, and Escobar was grinning as he turned away. It was one of the things he loved about this place. Everyone had a life story to tell, and everyone wanted to live that other life to see what new challenges were thrown at them. No life experience was wasted. Everything was up for grabs.

Escobar pondered all this as he walked slowly home to a meal with Rachel, Sarah, and his son Daniel the Younger.

CHAPTER 25.

65-70 AD

Luke turned away from the scene of the crucifixion and the beheading.

His heart was heavy. It was though he had been laden with heavy stones. The crowds had been silent, watching the final spasms of the man on the cross. A thunderous roar lashed across the sky as the two men died. Neither figure heard it. Paul's headless corpse lay near the foot of the cross. His Roman citizenship had in the end prevented his crucifixion, but he was still doomed to die.

A new determination was filling Luke. He felt like a historian on the brink of a great discovery. Gone was the frivolous nature of his work. His new works would embody the story of Christianity. A path of words for man to follow to reach true salvation. Paul and Petros had inspired him. Men like Escobar had filled in the details that would help give his work credence and credibility. He remembered the gift he had received as a child from the Seer, a book by Pliny the Elder, that outlined how the Essenes' movement had lived.

He thought of the sacrifices men and women had made down through the ages.

How they'd laid their lives down for God. He thought of all the prophets and of how each in their own imitable way had been persecuted for their faith. He could sense a divide in time and knew and sensed that his work would embody a New Testament for man to follow as distinct from the old one passed down through different generations.

But he wanted to go further. A gospel was fine, yes. But he also intended writing about the new spread of Christianity, the men who had inspired his thinking on the subject since the death of Jesus some fifty years before. He prayed that the Almighty would give him the time he needed to finish his works. He would call this aspect of his work the Acts of the Apostles. He hoped that it would gain as much credence as his gospel. The framework for the document was already entrusted to papyrus and parchment, but he needed time to adjust the chronology of the events and to make it a coherent whole. His reed pens and ink pots would see much use. It would require years of diligence.
But he knew in his heart he was ready to commit.
He had been blessed to live through these tumultuous times.
A true scribe!

*　*　*

Luke had returned to Greece.
Under the hot sun that habitually shone on Greece, he settled down to write his gospel.
It was only in this gospel that the story of the Annunciation came out. The visit of Mary to her cousin Elizabeth in Ein Karem had been carefully noted by Luke, who recorded everything like a true historian. His writings had an immediacy that wasn't apparent in the works of other gospel writers.
Although he had started compiling notes for his manuscript years ago, this was to be his final draft. He had retired as a physician and the extra time helped him to develop his work.
He worked tirelessly and diligently and often late into the night. He consulted his notes often, copiously checking facts and watching out for inconsistencies in his work.
His work included not only a new gospel, but another work which he titled the Acts of the Apostles. He also translated other works into Greek including the Epistle to the Hebrews. The Epistle to the Hebrews used Old Testament quotations interpreted in light of first century rabbinical Judaism. When

Luke asked Paul who had penned the document, Paul had appeared evasive.

"You don't need to know that," he was told. "Just translate it into Greek."

Luke had taken the reprimand in silence, but in truth he couldn't understand why there was such secrecy surrounding the authorship. He felt sure that future generations wouldn't thank them for harbouring secrets. He wondered had Paul himself written the document, which would have made it a Pauline document, but there was no way of knowing for sure if Paul didn't want to talk about it.

And that begged the question. Why did he not want to discuss it? Luke pondered on that, and his mind eventually settled on a probable reason. Paul had many friends, but one couple were close to him. He had lived with them for some time, and they shared a common thread in that they were all tentmakers. Priscilla and Aquila accompanied Paul on many of his trips, and that was how Luke knew them, but he suddenly remembered Priscilla writing one day when they were aboard a ship but when he had asked her about it, she had gone coy. He knew she was an eloquent speaker, along with her husband Aquila, and he wondered did that eloquence extend to whatever it had been that she was writing.

He had a feeling that it did translate, but he wouldn't ask Paul about it again. Perhaps he felt the need to protect Priscilla, and in fact the more he thought about it, the more he realised that this must be so. It said much for Paul's way of thinking that he would go to such great lengths to protect a friend and it showed why many were willing to show him vast loyalty.

By the time he had settled down to write the final drafts, he found he had plenty of time on his hands. Both of his parents had by now passed away, and his one remaining sister still lived in Toledo. He still received and sent letters to her, but most family contact was now a thing of the past.

He hadn't married himself; so, there were no distractions there. He felt lucky to be alive and to have witnessed everything that he

was about to write about. He remembered the words of the Seer explaining how his words would resonate through the ages and he felt the weight of responsibility on his shoulders. He settled down to write.
A true scribe!

CHAPTER 26.

81-96 AD

Ioanna saw a duty upon himself to correct things that the church may have been doing wrong. In this he had been enlightened by men like Luke whose gifts for writing could help steer the church through any doubts surfacing in the minds of people. Even at this early stage of the church, John recognised that schisms could arise. A number of years had passed since the crucifixion and knowing the nature of man and his ability for conflict and arguments, John decided to get words on paper that would help maintain a line in the sand. A path for Christians to follow. He knew man sometimes deciphered things the way they wanted them to, even though this deciphering might not be the way. It was important that the church didn't sway and distort the message that Christ had preached. Time and fading memories could distort all truths. He recognised that his own views on Christianity were different to the three gospel writers whose work he was most familiar with. Matthew, Mark, and Luke. He was also aware of other gospel writers - men like Judas and Thomas. And there were others.

He no longer lived in Ephesus but had instead being banished to the Greek island of Patmos, following a new crackdown on Christians by the Roman Emperor Domitian.

He didn't care.

He was surprised at his longevity.

Patmos was a small Greek island in the Aegean Sea, one of the most northern in the Dodecanese chain. Steeped in mythology the island was purportedly given as a present from Zeus to his daughter Artemis, the goddess of hunting. Though used by the Romans as a place of exile, Ioanna quite liked the peace and tranquillity of the little island. It was surrounded by turquoise-coloured waters.

He wasn't alone in his exile. He was gratified to discover that one of the seventy disciples specially appointed by Jesus to go out and preach the good news, Prochorus, was with him on the island. He made a mental note to contact the man, known for his heavenly singing, and known too as a scribe and a chronicler of events. He had also heard that the mystical figure of the Seer was here on Patmos, but that he had been consigned to hard labour in the salt mines.

However, the Romans obviously decided that his infirm age was proving a hindrance rather than a help, and they released the Seer from work duties.

He was left free to wander the island and that was how Ioanna met him. The Seer was sitting on a rock overlooking the Aegean, his weathered face pensive as he gazed out over the water, when Ioanna came upon him.

The Seer spoke first. "Views, I never tire of," he said, reflectively. "The sea...somehow it has a timeless quality about it. Don't you agree? Without waiting for a response, the Seer looked up at him. "You're Ioanna?"

"I am," Ioanna replied. "And you're the Seer?"

The old man acknowledged his head. The burden of living spoke through the visible bones of his hands, his skeletal frame, and his slow movements. Ioanna was still talking.

"You've lived a long life."

"Too long," the Seer admitted ruefully.

"Prochorus is here on Patmos," Ioanna commented.

The Seer brightened.

"Does he still sing beautifully?"

"As always."

Ioanna put another question to the mystic. "Do you think the gospels will stand the test of time?"

The Seer didn't answer immediately. His eyes clouded over as though he were trying to see far into the future. "I think they will," he confirmed. "At least certain ones. There will be four

main ones - Matthew, Mark and Luke."
"And the fourth?"
"Yours."
"What's your favourite one?"
"Luke. Without a shadow of doubt."
"How come?"
"There's an immediacy to his writings...perhaps, I'm prejudiced...I knew him when he was growing up...I remember when he was born...he always knew he wanted to write and paint...then as he got older, and especially after his family moved to Greece, he decided to pursue formal training and become a physician. You knew him, didn't you?"
Ioanna nodded. "Yes, he stayed in our community in Ephesus for several months, before accompanying the mother of Jesus back to Jerusalem."
"And then he followed Paul?"
"Yes. He returned to Greece following Paul's death in Rome. He stayed with him right to the very end. Did you ever hear his story of that event?"
"Story?"
"Seemingly when Paul was beheaded...he died on the same day as Petros..."
"Petros was crucified, wasn't he?"
"Yes, but they couldn't crucify Paul. He was a Roman citizen. So, they decided to behead him...Nero's madness. Anyway, according to Luke when they beheaded him, he didn't bleed blood, but milk."
"MILK?" The Seer was astonished.
"Milk," Ioanna insisted.
"Life is so strange," the Seer remarked. "Don't you agree?"
Ioanna nodded. "I've often felt that way," he agreed.
They heard somebody approaching, singing.
The Seer smiled. "Prochorus?"
"Who else," Ioanna remarked, smiling back.
The singing was heavenly and melodious and in-tune. The man himself came into view from around a headland; no pause in the

singing despite seeing the two men in front of him. He knew them both.

Prochorus was a small man in stature, but he had a big voice. He was a nephew of Stephen - the protomartyr. He had been appointed by the apostles back in Jerusalem as one of seven deacons with special responsibility for widows and the poor. The other six included Stephen, the protomartyr, Philip the Evangelist, Nicanor, Timon, Parmenas, and Nicholas. Some said that they were also part of the seventy disciples sent out by Jesus to spread the Word. Whatever the truth of that, it was easy to see that Prochorus was a man steeped with the Holy Spirit. His face was kind, as were his pale blue eyes. He too was a scribe.

It was a time that heralded the birth of the gospels.

A number of years went by, and Ioanna was finally freed from Patmos. He returned to Ephesus, and he worked away in a little cottage he had been given. It was small and compact, but it suited his lifestyle. He worked night and day on his gospel until one afternoon when he laid down his quill and reflected, his mind turned inward as though in prayer. Patmos was now a distant memory, and friends like Prochorus had gone to their heavenly reward. He smiled as he thought of the man now singing his heart out with the angels in heaven and proclaiming God. Even the Seer had gone the way of all mortal men and had finally succumbed in his old age.

Ioanna breathed in the warm, still air and he nodded to himself, feeling very alive. From what the Seer had once said to him he knew his writings would stand the test of time. It was an enjoyable time to be alive. He could feel the hot orb of the sun on his face.

He knew his purpose on earth. He knew he was here to chronicle events. He knew he was here to witness.

He knew he was here to write. Like Luke, he too was a true scribe!

THE END.

ABOUT THE AUTHOR

Liam Robert Mullen

Irish writer whose works including The Soaring Spirit, Kolbe, The Briefcase Men, Wings, Digger, and Land of Our Father. Latest works include The Scribe and The Nationalists and War. Further works include Orphans, Sorting out Charlie, Pacific Deeps, Atlantic Deeps, Arctic Deeps, Bio and Mano. Some of my stories have appeared on Wattpad to help gauge reader reaction before self-publication. As a writer one of the key advantages to self-publication is the ability to work on what I want, when I want, and I refuse to be pigeonholed into a certain category. I'm a writer that likes working across different genres and my reading reflects that kind of thinking too. Some of my stories were begun with novels in mind but ran out of steam and were published either as a long short story or as a novella.

The writer has a profile on www.writing.ie and blogs at freelancer555@wordpress.com

Can also be found on facebook@irishwriter112

PRAISE FOR AUTHOR

Escobar is a young member of the Sanhedrin when we meet him who has been persuaded to condemn Jesus and bitterly regrets it. He is also grieving his dead wife and child. His spiritual journey begins here. Refusing to help Caiphas to round up the new Christians, he makes contact with Peter – Petrus – who advises him to go to Ephesus to meet Mary, the mother of Jesus, who went there with John (Ioanna).

We follow Luke's story from his birth. Mullen gives him an unusual birth circumstance. He was well-educated and became a physican. His travels were well known and it is also thought that he received the Nativity story from Mary herself. Mullen makes this plausible by having Luke escort Mary back to Jerusalem from Ephesus toward the end of her life on earth.

I loved this book. I was very pleased when the story moved to Ephesus and to the house of Mary, which I was actually in about 30 years ago and was a very memorable experience, so it got personal for me. It was good to hear Ephesus described as she and St. John must have experienced, a busy seaport, bustling markets, overlooked by quiet hills (where Mary's House still is today).

Mullen's descriptions throughout are clear and vivid, and of course I love every writer who tell me what people eat and drink!

Sometimes the book took on a narrative form such as a very interesting chapter on how travellers prepared for a caravan. Instead of weaving it into the story, Mullen explains it to the reader. I don't see this as incorrect, 19th century writers often addressed the reader directly, and one does not have to follow 'rules' in a novel, except not to confuse the reader, and the only quibble about 'The Scribe' is that it jumps around a bit too much, though Mullen is careful to tell us the dates. It also felt too modern in dialogue and in some scenes. But I found these to be minor distractions, the overall experience was very enjoyable and informative, and I know more than I knew before about the immediate aftermath of the Resurrection. There are two Scribes in this work, John and Luke, writers of two of the four Gospels. This is a keeper. It's very rich in information about the early Church. The writer did a great deal of work and research. I can see myself re-reading it.

- MARY TERESA

BOOKS BY THIS AUTHOR

The Nationalists

Anyone interested in Irish history will enjoy The Nationalists, a story with a backdrop of the 1916 Rising, the War of Independence and the Irish Civil War. The story opens with Tony McAnthony meeting Angela O'Sullivan in the GPO during the Rising. Imprisoned after the Rising, Tony must fight for the woman he loves. He is forced to make hard, life-changing choices when Lucy, Angela's best friend, is raped by the Black and Tans, the hated British auxiliary forces. Tony must now make a choice between the pen and the gun. Angela is taken aback by what he decides and as a headstrong Kerry woman she goes her own way. Their paths will collide again later. Father John Troy also has difficult choices to make. His decision to render aid to rebels lands him in prison and on a collision course with Rome, the Irish hierarchy and fellow priests. The Rising, of course, was more than a military thing. A cultural revolution took place in tandem. The Nationalists explores this aspect as well including the Abbey Theatre. The story interweaves factual and fictional characters - men like Eamon de Valera and Michael Collins. The story isn't completely set in Dublin but moves to Kerry, Wales and London and moves on from the Rising to the elections of 1918, the Black and Tan War and the Irish Civil War. Everyone is affected. Nobody escapes unscathed.

Orphans

Orphans - a Larry Lir mystery. An Irish boy with dark, magical powers.

Who couldn't help but be inspired by the phenomenal success of the Harry Potter series? I got the idea for Orphans from this, but I wanted an Irish character, and I wanted a story rooted in Celtic mythology, legend and myth; and I wanted to combine all these elements into a modern setting that children could enjoy. I wanted to incorporate modern technology, modern forensics, and modern thinking into a spellbinding tale for children and in Larry Lir, I think I found that character. Larry is a twelve year old who fends mostly for himself in a rambling mansion on the Hill of Howth, in Dublin.

Orphans is, I believe, aptly titled. The main character, Larry is left an orphan following the brutal murder of his parents. When three Cuban children, recently orphaned themselves, appeal to Larry for help, he has to take up their case. The shadow of Charles Dickens and the splendid Oliver Twist looms a bit here. Even his archenemy is an orphan.

There is an important underlying message in the book that relates to basic press freedom and democratic values. The Book is set for the most part in Ireland, both in Dublin and Wexford. Other locations used are the USA and Cuba.

There are strong hints of mythology like the famous fable of Oisin, warned not to dismount from his horse when he returned to Irish soil lest the years catch up with him.

The Children of Lir, of whom Larry is a direct descendent, also play a role in this tale. A curse from their time hangs over Larry. A short extract from Orphans is given here:

Lir knew how to play on their fears.
He knew Quique was terrified of snakes, that Da Silva had nightmares about the man he had killed when he was twelve,

and that certain things could unsettle Julio too. It was the power of the black magic within him that enabled him to play on these fears, but it was a power he preferred not to utilise because it could leave him feeling drained and powerless.

The book shows, I hope, the independent spirit that dwells within children and the battle of triumph over evil.

Sorting Out Charlie

Charlie Evans is a troubled teenager living in Gorey, Co Wexford. When he falls foul of the law, his parents take radical action and pack him off to India for a year's schooling.
At first, he rebels against this treatment. Removed from his comfort zone, he continues getting into trouble. Slowly however, he settles into his new way of life in India. He befriends a boy of his own age, who introduces him to the world of cricket, and he falls for Sharu, his new friend's sister.
Ultimately this YA story is about a coming to age, young love, and a growing passion for sport.

War

From the author of The Nationalists and The Scribe comes War, a mix of action and war stories, some with an Irish slant like The Pitboys, a tale of two young Irish lads working the coalmines of Tipperary at a time of great social upheaval - the Young Irelander rebellion and the Irish famine. Many of the stories are told from the perspective of the Second World War, but not exclusively so. Stories about modern conflicts also surface - the Gulf War, the Yugoslavia conflict and the Israeli and Palestinian conflicts.
In a time of War, nobody's innocent.

Mano

Mano.

There's a new cop in Hawaii, and he doesn't take prisoners. This is the tagline which I've used for Mano, a tough cop in Hawaii whose brief includes keeping terrorism out of Hawaii.

The tale is a post 911 piece and concerns the hunt for an ISIS terrorist cell intent on carrying out a dirty bomb attack on the USS Arizona memorial at Pearl Harbour. The group is led by the fanatical Hakim, a Saudi terrorist who used to work as an executioner in his home country.

When he finds out that there is a tough cop called Mano out to stop him, he makes a near fatal error of judgement by ordering a hit on one of Hawaii's top cops - a move that will bring in the FBI and Homeland Security - and makes Mano aware of the threat against him. Mano is already a marked man because of his previous undercover work on the Chinese triads. His security detail has always been aware of threats made against him and are constantly in a heightened state of alert anyway.

Mano has the cream of HPD already working within his squad, besides his own security detail, experienced cops like The Seeker, Nui, and Pono. Together they form a formidable team which Hakim will have trouble overcoming.

The story carries a lot of pace and action and strong characterization which ultimately will propel the story forward to a nail-biting conclusion.

Daniel Norrish of Indie Ebook Uprising says of Mano: "A badass Hawaiian cop who becomes the island's best defense against the onslaught of terrorism."

Printed in Poland
by Amazon Fulfillment
Poland Sp. z o.o., Wrocław
04 July 2022

54a405c9-b74a-4e61-af94-3d1268738a1dR01